THE ATLANTIS REVELATION

Also by Thomas Greanias

The Atlantis Prophecy
Raising Atlantis

THE
ATLANTIS
REVELATION

Thomas Greanias

ATRIA BOOKS

New York   London   Toronto   Sydney

ATRIA BOOKS
A Division of Simon & Schuster, Inc.
1230 Avenue of the Americas
New York, NY 10020

First Atria Books hardcover edition August 2009

ATRIA BOOKS and colophon are trademarks of Simon & Schuster, Inc.

For information about special discounts for bulk purchases, please contact Simon & Schuster Special Sales at 1-866-506-1949 or business@simonandschuster.com.

The Simon & Schuster Speakers Bureau can bring authors to your live event. For more information or to book an event, contact the Simon & Schuster Speakers Bureau at 1-866-248-3049 or visit our website at www.simonspeakers.com.

Designed by Peng Olaguera
Map courtesy of the author

Manufactured in the United States of America

10 9 8 7 6 5 4 3 2 1

Library of Congress Cataloging-in-Publication Data

Greanias, Thomas.
    The Atlantis revelation / by Thomas Greanias. —1st Atria Books hardcover ed.
        p. cm.
    1. Archaeologists—Fiction. 2. Atlantis (Legendary place)—Fiction.
    3. Conspiracies—Fiction.   I. Title.
    PS3607.R4286A96 2009
    813'.6—dc22

                                                        2009013275

ISBN 978-1-4165-8912-9
ISBN 978-1-4165-9746-9 (ebook)

Once again, for Laura

A river watering the garden flowed from Eden. . . . And the LORD God said, "The man has now become like one of us, knowing good and evil. He must not be allowed to reach out his hand and take also from the tree of life and eat, and live forever." So the LORD God banished him from the Garden of Eden to work the ground from which he had been taken. After he drove the man out, he placed on the east side of the Garden of Eden cherubim and a flaming sword flashing back and forth to guard the way to the tree of life.

—Genesis 2:10, 3:22–24

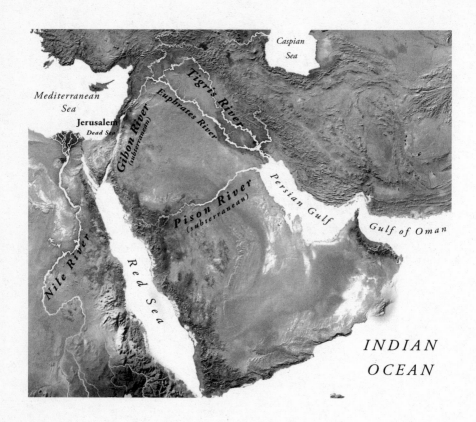

PART ONE

Corfu

1

The Calypso Deep
Ionian Sea

Conrad Yeats started having second thoughts as soon as they anchored the fishing boat *Katrina* over the discovery.

It wasn't just that he hated the water. Or that it was three miles to the bottom at the deepest part of the Mediterranean. Or that his Greek crew believed these waters were cursed. It was the words of a former U.S. secretary of defense warning that what Conrad sought didn't exist, but if it did, he was not to disturb it or else. *Maybe it's time you gave it a rest, son, and let the damned past rust in peace.*

But he had come too far on his journey to recover a real-world relic from the mythological lost continent of Atlantis to turn back now. And he would never rest until he found out exactly what kind of damned past everyone would just as soon bury simply because it threatened their own vision of the future.

Conrad pulled the black neoprene wet suit over his shoulders and looked over at Stavros, his diving attendant. The big, strapping Greek had hauled up the sonar towfish that a team of side-scan sonar experts from the exploration ship had used to get a fix on the target only hours ago. Now he was fiddling with Conrad's air compressor.

"You finally fix that thing?" Conrad asked.

Stavros grunted. "Think so."

Conrad glanced up at Polaris, the brightest star in the constellation Ursa Major, and then at the silvery waters. This location wasn't on any charts. He'd found it by using ancient poems, ships' logs, and astronomical data that only an astro-archaeologist like himself would take seriously.

Yet he wasn't alone.

The black cutout of a megayacht loomed on the dark horizon. For a pleasure palace cruising the Ionian Islands on an Easter holiday vacation, the six-hundred-foot vessel boasted an impressive communications array, a helicopter, and for all Conrad knew, even a couple of submersibles. It was probably all for show, but Conrad still didn't like someone else with that kind of firepower near his find.

He planned to be long gone before the sun came up. "I need forty minutes of air to the bottom and back," he told Stavros.

Stavros threw out a small buoy tied to two hundred meters of line. "If she's still sitting on the edge of the trench, like the robotic camera showed, you'll be lucky to get twenty minutes of bottom time," Stavros said. "If she's slipped into the Calypso, then it doesn't matter. The Baron of the Black Order himself will grab you by the leg and drag you down to hell." He shivered and made the sign of the cross over his heart.

Conrad could do without a Greek chorus to remind him that tragedy haunted these waters. In the light of day, the surface of the Ionian was among the most serene for sailing in Greece, surrounded by easy anchorages and safe bays for cruise ships and private yachts alike. But in the darkness of its depths was one of the most seismic areas in the world.

There, three miles down at the bottom of the Hellenic Trench, lay the vast Calypso Deep. It was the point where the African tectonic plate subducted the Eurasian plate, pulling anything too close under the plates and into the earth's magma. Even, some had argued, something as big as a continent.

"You worry about my oxygen, Stavros. I'll worry about the curse of the Calypso." Conrad slipped on his full-face dive mask and stepped off the bow, fins first, into the sea.

The cool water enveloped him as he followed the anchored buoy line to the bottom. His high-powered Newtlite head lantern illuminated the way through the darkness. Halfway down he met a school of bottlenose dolphins. They parted like a curtain to reveal the startling sight of the legendary *Nausicaa* rising out of the depths, her 37mm antiaircraft guns pointing straight at him.

The German submarine was imposing enough, which Conrad had expected. After all, it had belonged to SS General Ludwig von Berg—the Baron of the Black Order, as he was known to his friends in the Third Reich. Among other things, the baron was head of Hitler's Ahnenerbe, an organization of academics, philosophers, and military warriors sent to scour the earth to prove the Aryans were the descendants of Atlantis.

That mission had taken Baron von Berg as far away as Antarctica, where decades later, Conrad's father, USAF General Griffin Yeats, had uncovered a secret Nazi base and ancient ruins two miles beneath the ice. But any evidence of that lost civiliza-tion—Atlantis—was wiped away in a seismic event that killed his father, sank an ice shelf the size of California, and may well have caused the Indian Ocean tsunami of 2004 that killed thousands in Indonesia.

Ever since, Conrad had been trying to find some proof that what he had found under Antarctica wasn't a dream. Clues left by his father on his tombstone at Arlington Cemetery had told Conrad as much and more. Soon he had discovered that his father's succes-sor as head of the Pentagon's DARPA research and development agency, Max Seavers, had developed a weaponized flu virus from the infected lung tissue of dead Nazis found frozen in Antarctica.

Those discoveries ultimately led Conrad to the mysterious Baron von Berg. Classified American, British, and German intel-ligence files from World War II recorded that the SS general's U-boat, *Nausicaa*, was returning from its secret base in Antarctica when it was sunk by the British Royal Navy in 1943.

Conrad's hope was that he would find on board a relic from Atlantis.

He kicked through the water toward the sunken submarine. The *Nausicaa* lay like a gutted whale along the cusp of the Calypso Deep with her tail broken off and her forward section jutting out over the abyss like a metal coffin.

Conrad swam to the mouth of the broken fuselage and stud-ied its teeth. The British torpedo that had sunk the *Nausicaa* had taken out the entire electric motor room. But it wasn't a clean break. One little nick of his air hose would cut off his oxygen. He spoke into his dive helmet's integrated radio. "Stavros."

"Right here, boss," the Greek's voice crackled in his earpiece.

"How's the compressor?"

"Still ticking, boss."

Conrad swam into the abandoned control room of the forward section, keeping his eyes peeled for floating skeletons. He found none. No diving officers, helmsmen, or planesmen. Not even in the conning tower. Just an empty compartment with unmanned banks of instruments to his port and starboard sides. Had all hands managed to abandon ship before she went down?

The captain's quarters were empty, too. There was only a phonograph with a warped album. Conrad could still read the peeling label on the album: *Die Walküre.* Von Berg had been playing Wagner's "Ride of the Valkyries" over the loudspeakers when the sub went down.

But no sign of Baron von Berg himself. Nor a metallic Kriegsmarine briefcase. Maybe the legend was true, and von Berg never carried secret papers with him, telling everyone instead: "It's all in my head."

Conrad's hopes of finding anything were sinking fast.

He swam up the cramped fore-and-aft passageway through the galley and officers' quarters. A creeping claustrophobia washed over him as he slipped through the open hatch into the forward torpedo bay.

At one end were four circular hatches—the torpedo tubes. The atmospheric pressure gauges, frozen in time, told him that the *Nausicaa* had fired off at least three torpedos and drained her tubes to fire more when the Brits sank her. Only the No. 4 tube was flooded. The Baron of the Black Order obviously had not gone down without a fight.

Conrad turned to the bomb racks and found a large protrusion. He fanned away the accumulated silt. An object took form, and he realized he was staring at a human skull with black holes for eyes.

The bared teeth seemed to grin at him in the eerie deep. The skull had a silver plate screwed into one side—the legacy of a bullet to the head in Crete, Conrad had learned in his research.

SS General Ludwig von Berg. The Baron of the Black Order. The rightful king of Bavaria. That was what the old top-secret OSS report Conrad had stolen had said.

Conrad felt a shock wave in the water, and the *Nausicaa* seemed to lurch.

"Stavros!" he called into his radio, but there was no response.

Suddenly, the black holes in the baron's skull glowed a bright red, and his skeletal arm floated up as if to grab Conrad.

Conrad backed away from the skeleton, figuring that the water was playing tricks on him. Then he noticed that the glow actually came from something behind the skull. Indeed, the Baron of the Black Order seemed to be guarding something.

Conrad's heart pounded as he brushed away more silt, revealing an odd hammerhead-shaped warhead. He shined a light on it and ran his hands across the torpedo's slick casing.

It had no markings save for a code name stamped across the warhead's access panel: *Flammenschwert*. Conrad's rudimentary grasp of German translated it to mean "Flaming Sword" or "Sword of Fire."

He recalled from his research that von Berg claimed to have developed a weapon that the Nazis were convinced could win them the war: an incendiary technology that allegedly was Atlantean in origin and could turn water into fire and even melt the ice caps.

Could this be the relic he was searching for that would prove Antarctica was Atlantis?

The mysterious glow was coming from inside the hammer-head cone of the torpedo, outlining the square access panel like a neon light. But this was no mere illumination. The light seemed to be consuming the water around the warhead like a fire consumes oxygen.

Conrad's dosimeter gauge registered no radiation, so he put the fingertip of his glove to the glowing seam of the access panel. It didn't burn his glove, but he could feel an unmistakable pull. The warhead was sucking in the water around it like a black hole.

He sensed another shock wave through the water and turned to see four shadowy figures with harpoon guns enter the torpedo bay.

They must be after the *Flammenschwert*! he thought. He'd rather sink the sub than let this weapon fall into anybody's hands.

He reached up for the blow valves above the four torpedo tubes and twisted the wheels, flooding three of them. The sub tilted forward toward the Calypso Deep, throwing the others back. The rumbling was deafening. Breathing hard in his mask, heaving as he kicked, he was swimming madly to escape the torpedo bay when a harpoon dart stabbed his thigh.

Grimacing in pain, Conrad grabbed his leg as three of the divers swarmed around him. He broke off the harpoon dart and stabbed in the gut the diver who had shot him. The diver doubled over as a cloud of blood billowed out of his wet suit. The other two had grabbed him, however, and before Conrad could tear away, their leader swam over, drew a dagger, and sliced through Conrad's lifeline.

Conrad watched in shock as silver bubbles rose up before his eyes like a Roman candle, literally taking his breath away.

Then he saw the dagger again, this time its butt smashing the glass of his mask. Water began filling the mask, and he inhaled some against his will. His life flashed by in a blur—his father the Griffter, his childhood in Washington, D.C., his digs around the world searching for Earth's lost "mother culture," meeting Serena in South America, then Antarctica . . .

Serena.

His lips tried to repeat the prayer that Serena had taught him, the last prayer of Jesus: "Into Thy hands I commit my spirit." But the words refused to come. He could only see her face, now fading away. Then darkness.

When Conrad opened his eyes again, the phantom divers were gone. He wasn't breathing, but his lungs weren't filled with water, either—laryngospasm had sealed his airway. He would suffocate instead of drowning if he didn't surface immediately.

He looked out through his shattered dive mask to see the skull of SS General Ludwig von Berg smiling at him. The fire had gone out of the baron's eyes. Also gone was the *Flammenschwert* warhead, along with the shadow divers. But the divers had left behind something for him: a brick of C4 explosive with a digital display slapped next to the torpedo's open casing.

The numbers read: 2:43 . . . 2:42 . . . 2:41 . . .

On top of the C4 was a metal ball bearing that glowed like a burning ember from hell. It must have been extracted from the *Flammenschwert,* which probably contained thousands of these copperlike pellets inside its core. The bastards were going to verify the design by detonating just one tiny pellet, simulating on a small scale the device's explosive power. In the process, they were going to destroy him and the *Nausicaa.*

Conrad mustered the last of his strength and tried to swim out, but his leg caught on something—the skeletal hand of SS General Ludwig von Berg. The baron, it seemed, wanted to drag him to hell.

Conrad couldn't break free. The clock was down to 1:33.

Thinking quickly, he grabbed the baron's steel-plated skull with both hands and broke it off the skeleton. Slipping his fingers into the eyeholes as if the skull were a bowling ball, he brought it down on the finger bones clasping his injured leg and smashed them to pieces.

He was free, but his fingers were now stuck like a claw through the skull as another shock wave hit the *Nausicaa.*

The entire forward torpedo bay dropped like a broken table—silt and debris sliding past him to the front, further tipping the submarine over the edge of the Calypso Deep. Conrad's back slammed against the bomb rack, and he saw the compartment hatch and entire fore-aft passageway beyond rising like a great elevator shaft above him.

The *Nausicaa* was about to go down nose-first into the Calypso. Conrad had only seconds left. He positioned himself under the hatch, forcing himself to resist the temptation to panic. He held his body ramrod-straight, like a torpedo, his hands arched together with the skull over his head. Then he closed his eyes as everything collapsed around him.

For a moment he felt like a missile shooting up out of its silo, although he knew it was the silo that was sinking. Then he was clear. He looked down into the Calypso Deep as it swallowed the *Nausicaa* with the tiny pellet from the *Flammenschwert* still inside its belly.

The powerful wake of the plunging sub began to pull him down like a vertical riptide. He knew if he fought it, he'd go down with it. Instead he made long scissor kicks across the wake and over the rim of the crater, putting as much distance between him and the abyss as possible. There was a flash of light behind him, and the water suddenly heated up.

Conrad looked back over his shoulder in time to see a giant pillar of fire shoot straight up from the depths of the Calypso. The sound of thunder rippled across the deep. Abruptly, the flames fanned out and seemed to assume the form of a dragon flying through the water toward him. Conrad started swimming as fast as he could.

He surfaced a minute later into the dim predawn light of day, gasping for breath. Finally, as he was on the verge of passing out again forever, his larynx opened, and he coughed up a little water from his stomach as he desperately inhaled the salty air.

His groan sounded like jet engines in his own ears. He was sure he was experiencing some kind of pulmonary embolism from coming up so fast. Several deep gulps of air cleared his head enough for him to scan the horizon for his boat. But it wasn't there. In the distance loomed the silhouette of a megayacht, its decks stacked like gold bullion in the glint of the rising sun, turning away.

Debris floated around him—the remains of his boat. Poor Stavros, he thought. He swam toward a broken wooden plank to use for flotation. But when he got there, he realized it wasn't wood at all. It was the charred carcass of a bottlenose dolphin, burned to a crisp.

The horrific nature of the *Flammenschwert* sank in.

It works. It really turns water to fire.

Conrad stared at the dolphin's blackened rostrum and teeth. He felt some stomach acid rising at the back of his own throat and looked away. All around him were incinerated bottlenose dolphins, floating like driftwood across a sea of death.

2

Sister Serena Serghetti clutched the metal box containing African rice seeds to her chest as she walked down a long tunnel blasted out of the arctic mountain. High above her, fluorescent lights flashed on and off as she passed embedded motion detectors. Close behind, a choir of Norwegian schoolchildren held candles in the flickering darkness and sang "Sleep Little Seedling."

Their heavenly voices felt heavy in the freezing air, Serena thought, weighted perhaps by the tunnel's meter-thick walls of reinforced concrete. Or maybe it was her heart that felt so heavy.

The Doomsday Vault, as it was called when it opened in 2008, already housed more than two million seeds representing every variety of the earth's crops. In time it would house a collection of a hundred million seeds from more than 140 countries here on this remote island near the North Pole. It had been built to protect the world's food supply against nuclear war, climate change, terrorism, rising sea levels, earthquakes, and the ensuing collapse of power supplies. If worse came to worst, the vault would allow the world to reconstruct agriculture on the planet.

But now the vault itself was in danger. Thanks to global warming, the shrinking ice caps had spurred a new race for oil in the Arctic. It was the next Saudi Arabia, if someone could figure out a way to extract and transport all that oil through a sea of ice. A few years earlier, the Russians had even planted a flag two and a half miles below the ice at the North Pole to claim its oil reserves. Now Serena feared they were preparing to start mining.

She passed through two separate air locks and into the vault itself, blinking into the glare of the TV lights. The Norwegian prime minister was in there somewhere, along with a delegation from the United Nations.

Serena knelt before the TV cameras and prayed silently for the people of the earth. But she was aware of shutters clicking and photographers' boots shuffling for better shots of her.

Whatever happened to finding a secret place to pray, like Jesus taught? she wondered, unable to shake a guilty feeling. Did the world really need to see Mother Earth arrayed in high-definition piety 24/7? As if the prayers of the Vatican's top linguist and environmental czar counted more than those of the anonymous humble field laborer whose hands culled the seeds she now held.

But this was a cause greater than herself and her tormented thirty-three-year-old soul, she reminded herself. And her official purpose here today was to focus the world's attention on its future.

As she knelt, tightly gripping the box of seeds, a feeling of dread came over her. What the vault meant, what it was built for: the time of the end, which the Bible had prophesied would come soon. The words of the prophet Isaiah whispered in her ear: God is the only God. He will draw all people to Himself to see His glory. He will end this world. And He will judge those who reject Him.

Not something TV audiences wanted to hear.

She felt a nagging sense of hypocrisy about her performance. A disturbing thought began to bubble up, a thought she couldn't quite formulate. Her dread began to take shape in the words of Jesus: "If therefore you are offering your gift at the altar, and there remember that your brother has anything against you, leave your gift there before the altar, and go your way. First be reconciled to your brother, and then come and offer your gift."

She didn't understand. She had plenty of people angry with her at the Vatican—for being a woman, for being beautiful, for drawing cameras wherever she went—and that was just within the Church. Outside, there were the oil and gas companies she chided, and diamond merchants, and the exploiters of children.

But that wasn't what this word from God was about.

Conrad Yeats.

She fought to push his face out of her mind and felt the slightest tremor as her knees pressed against the concrete floor.

That rogue? That liar, cheat, and thief? What could he possibly have against me? Other than I wouldn't sleep with him?

But she couldn't get his face—his handsome unshaved face—out of her mind. Nor could she forget how she had left things in Washington, D.C., a few years back, after he had saved her life. She had promised to leave the Church and be with him forever. Instead she had stolen something priceless out from under him and the U.S. government, leaving him with nothing.

But Lord, You know it was for Conrad's own good and the greater good.

When she opened her eyes and rose to her feet, she surrendered the box of African rice seeds to the Norwegian prime minister. With solemn fanfare, he opened the box for the cameras, revealing sealed silver packets, each labeled with a special bar code. Then he resealed the box and slid it onto its designated shelf in the vault.

After the ceremony, she went into the main tunnel and found her driver and bodyguard, Benito, waiting for her with her parka. She slipped it on, and they started walking toward the main entrance to the facility.

"Just as you suspected, *signorina*," he told her, handing her a small blue device. "Our divers found it at the bottom of the arctic seabed."

It was a geophone. Oil companies used them to take seismic surveys of the earth's subsurface in search of oil, in this case the earth two miles beneath the ice and water of the North Pole. Her visit to the Doomsday Vault had been a cover for her to meet with divers who could investigate for signs of drilling.

"So someone is planning to mine the bottom of the Arctic," she said, watching her breath freeze as they stood before the facility's dual blast-proof doors. Slowly and heavily, the doors opened.

The arctic air slapped Serena in the face as she stepped outside, where a van with tanklike treads was waiting to take her to the island's airport, the northernmost in the world with regular flights. Behind her, the exterior of the Doomsday Vault looked like something out of a science fiction movie, a giant granite wedge protruding from the ice.

The Norwegian island of Spitsbergen had been chosen as the location for the seed vault because it was a remote region with low tectonic activity and an arctic environment that was ideal for preservation. Now oil exploration posed a direct threat to this environment. It would also accelerate global warming's melting of the ice cap, threatening coastal cities around the world.

So why was she thinking of Conrad Yeats?

Something is terribly wrong, she thought. *He's in danger.*

But she couldn't put her finger on why and blamed her gloomy thoughts on the sweeping vista of endless ice and water spread out before her. It brought back memories of her adventure with Conrad in Antarctica years ago.

Benito said, "Our divers say there are thousands of them, maybe even tens of thousands, below us."

Serena realized he was talking about the geophone in her hand. "It will take them at least six months to map all the underground formations," she said. "So we still have some time before they decide where to start drilling. That might give us a chance to stop them."

"The Russians?" Benito asked.

"Maybe." She flipped the geophone over and saw the manufacturer's name: Midas Minerals & Mining LTD. "But I know who can tell us."

3

CORFU

If Sir Roman Midas loved anything in his life, it was his prized superyacht. Named after his one true love—himself—the *Midas* had a two-thousand-square-foot gym, two two-person submarines, and two helicopter pads, one for his chopper and one for guests. At 595 feet, the *Midas* was longer than the Washington Monument was high and, by design, resembled a shining stack of sliced gold bricks. Today those bricks sat atop the sparkling blue waters of the Ionian Sea near the Greek island of Corfu.

Not bad for a Russian orphan turned British tycoon, Roman Midaslovich told himself as he stood on the aft-deck helipad. He watched while a winch transferred the unmarked crate to the awaiting helicopter, its blades whirling for takeoff.

Midas's London-based trading firm, Midas Minerals & Mining, had made him the world's richest trader in minerals and metals futures, and his patronage to the art world had won him a knighthood from the queen. It had also made him a top lieutenant inside the Alignment, a centuries-old organization whose leaders fancied themselves the political if not the biological descendants of Atlantis. *Utter rubbish,* Midas had thought when he first heard the Alignment's claim to have orchestrated the rise and fall of empires across the ages. He alone was responsible for his rise from a Russian orphanage and the mines of Siberia to the trading pits of Chicago. But then the Alignment had orchestrated his entrée to the jet set of London and awarded him seats inside some of the international organizations that truly set the world's agenda: the Club of Rome, the Trilateral Commission, and the Bilderberg Group. Now he was a believer.

He waved off the pilot and watched the chopper lift into the sky. Then he turned to see Vadim Fedorov, his number two, standing before him in all his steroid-pumped muscularity. "They're waiting for you in the decompression chamber, sir," Vadim said.

"They" were two of the other divers from the *Nausicaa* extraction, Sergei and Yorgi. As far as everyone else was concerned, they were the only people who had seen the *Flammenschwert* besides himself and the pilot of the submersible, whom he had already dispatched to the ocean depths. Meanwhile, the helicopter would carry the crate to the airstrip on Corfu, and Midas's Gulfstream V private jet in turn would fly it to its intended destination.

"Is everything set?" Midas asked.

Vadim nodded. "You were right. They are FSB. Sergei sent a text message to Moscow almost immediately after they surfaced."

"They never really went away, you know."

Midas was speaking of Russia's ancient secret police, which, after the czars, had become the Soviet Union's feared KGB. After the collapse of the Soviet Union, Russia's first president, Boris Yeltsin, had dismantled the KGB and renamed it the Federal Security Service, or FSB.

Many deeply disillusioned agents, such as Sergei and Yorgi, had gone into the private security business, ultimately supplanting the mafia in running Russia's "protection" rackets. Others, such as Russia's former president and prime minister Vladimir Putin, had penetrated the government. Today in Russia, three out of four leading politicians boasted a background in the security forces, and almost every large Russian corporation was run by ex-KGB executives with personal ties to Putin.

Sergei and Yorgi, despite their employment agreements with Midas Minerals & Mining, were Putin's men and as such no longer of any use to Midas. "Tell them I'll be down in a moment. First I owe Sorath a progress report," Midas said. Vadim nodded.

Midas entered his stateroom and poured himself a drink while he waited for the coded signal to connect. Right now Sorath was just a code name to a voice on the other end of the phone. Midas had no idea who Sorath was or if they had ever met. But all his questions would be answered soon enough.

"This is Xaphan," Midas reported as soon as a light told him he was on a secure connection with Sorath. "The sword has been removed from its sheath and is en route to Uriel. A successful test has proved the design is safe for deployment and that the device's criticality formulas are correct."

"What of Semyaza?" the voice demanded, referring to Yeats.

"Dead."

"Those were not your orders." There was anger in the voice.

"It couldn't be helped," Midas said, and quickly moved on. "We're on schedule. T minus eight days."

"Keep it that way."

The line cut out, and Midas stared at the images of Conrad Yeats on the large flat-panel screen of his computer. He zoomed in on one in particular—of the archaeologist's DNA. There was nothing remarkable about it save for one thing: It spiraled to the left. All indigenous life on earth has DNA that spirals to the right. To the Alignment, that bestowed Yeats with some mystical meaning, as if the freak of nature somehow possessed some lost pieces of Atlantean blood in his genetic makeup.

Midas could care less. He closed the image on his screen and, with a few taps on his keyboard, connected with his trading firm mainframes in London. Then he went down to the lower decks and the yacht's submersible launch bay.

Next to a double-domed "deep flight" Falcon submarine, designed to fly underwater like a private jet through the air, was the decompression chamber, its hatch wide open, with Sergei and Yorgi waiting for him inside.

Yorgi didn't look too good, his stomach hastily patched where the late, great Dr. Yeats had stabbed him with his own harpoon dart.

"We could have been decompressing instead of waiting for you," Sergei complained. "Are you trying to kill us?"

Midas smiled, stepped inside the chamber, and allowed Vadim to close the hatch on the three of them. The air compressor started to hum and raise the internal air pressure to rid their bodies of harmful gas bubbles caused by inhaling oxygen at higher pressure during their dive for the *Flammenschwert.* The two divers were rubbing their itchy skin and sore joints. They were clearly displaying symptoms of the bends—their lungs alone were unable to expel the bubbles formed inside their bodies.

"I wanted us to decompress together," Midas said, taking his seat opposite the two FSB men. "But first I had to see off the *Flammenschwert.*"

Sergei and Yorgi looked at each other. "The arrangement was for us to take it back to Moscow," Sergei said.

"*Nyet,*" said Midas. "I have other plans for the *Flammenschwert,* and they don't involve the FSB."

"You are a dead man if you betray Moscow, Midaslovich," Sergei said. "Our organization spans the globe and is as old as the czars."

"Mine is older," Midas scoffed. "And now it has something yours does not—the power to turn oceans into fire."

"The deal was to use it in the Arctic and split the oil," Sergei pressed.

"Like the deal you did with British Petroleum in Russia before you stole their operations and ran them out?" Midas answered calmly as the air inside the chamber started to smell like bitter almonds. "Fools. Higher oil prices may have fueled your regime, but you don't know how to manage production. So you nationalize it and penalize real producers like me. Now that production has peaked, you have no choice but to stick your noses south into the Middle East and make war. You could have been kings instead of criminals."

Sergei and Yorgi began to cough and choke. Sergei said, "What have you done?"

Midas coughed twice. It would have been easier to throw them into the chamber, crank the dial, and blow their guts out. But it also would have been a mess to clean.

"As a child in the gold mines of Siberia, I was forced to extract gold from finely crushed ore," he told them calmly, like a firefighter lighting up a cigarette in the middle of an inferno. "Unfortunately, the only chemical up to the job is cyanide. It's stable when solid. But as a gas, it's toxic. I can see you are already experiencing rapid breathing, restlessness, and nausea."

Sergei began to vomit while Yorgi crumpled to the floor in convulsions.

"As for myself, my body developed a tolerance to the immediate effects of cyanide. But rest assured, I am experiencing all that you are to a lesser degree, and my doctors inform me that my long-term prognosis is the same as yours. We can't all live forever, can we?" Midas knew he didn't have to bother with theatrics in order to kill his enemies, but somehow he felt it was deeply important to show them that he had not only beaten them through his cleverness, but he was also, in his physical and mental evolution, inherently superior to them. "As your blood pressure lowers and heart rate slows, you will soon experience loss of consciousness, respiratory failure, and finally death. But you died a hero to the people. Too bad they are the wrong people."

The two were already dead by the time Midas had finished what passed for a eulogy. A minute later, he emerged from the chamber. The cyanide dispersed into the air, and two crewmen coughed. He left them to dispose of the bodies and took an elevator topside to the deck.

As he stepped into the sunlight and blinked, he reached for the sunglasses in his shirt pocket and glanced at his hand, which trembled slightly. It was the only visible neurological damage caused by his long-term exposure to cyanide poisoning as a child. So far.

He enjoyed watching death—it made him feel so alive. Like the salt that he now smelled in the sea air. Or the sight of Mercedes sunning topless in her chaise longue that he drank in on the foredeck. He made himself a vodka martini and stretched out next to her golden body, looking forward to tonight's party on Corfu and letting all thoughts of Nazi submarines and American archaeologists fade away like a bad late-night movie.

4

Conrad Yeats stared at the skull of SS General Ludwig von Berg inside his suite at the Andros Palace Hotel in Corfu town overlooking Garitsa Bay. The balcony doors were open wide, and a gentle early-evening breeze blew in, carrying with it music from the town green below.

He took another swig from his bottle of seven-star Metaxa brandy. His leg smarted from the harpoon dart, and his mind still reeled from the events of the morning: the *Flammenschwert*, the loss of Stavros and the crew, and the image of Serena Serghetti filling what he'd thought were his dying moments.

There was a knock at the door. Conrad put down his Metaxa, picked up a 9mm Glock from under the sofa pillow next to him, and stood up. He moved to the door and looked through the peephole.

It was Andros. Conrad opened the door, and his friend walked in. Two big security types with earpieces and shoulder holsters were posted outside.

"We have a problem," said Andros, closing the door behind him.

Chris Andros III, barely thirty, was always worried. A billionaire shipping heir, Andros had squandered several years after Harvard Business School dating American starlets and hotel heiresses from Paris Hilton to Ivanka Trump. Now a consummate international businessman, he was bent on making up for lost time and owned the Andros Palace Hotel, along with a string of high-end boutique hotels around the Mediterranean and the Middle East. It was Andros who had helped Conrad find the *Nausicaa*. Andros claimed the sub was named after his grandmother, who, as a young nurse in Nazi-occupied Greece, had been forced to help the Baron of the Black Order recover from his gunshot wound to the head.

"Let me guess," Conrad said. "That superyacht I saw belongs to Sir Roman Midas, and your friends at the airstrip have no idea what was on that private jet of his that took off today or where it was going."

Andros nodded and saw the laptop computer Conrad had used for his research sitting at the bar, its screen filled with news and images of Midas. He seemed about to say something else when he saw the skull of SS General Ludwig von Berg on the table. "That's him?"

"Silver plate and all."

Andros walked over and studied the skull and its metallic dome. He made the sign of the cross. "I cannot tell you how many nightmares this baron gave me growing up. My parents told me stories about what happened to those who crossed the baron—or children who didn't listen to their parents. Being a naughty boy myself, I had nightmares of his skull floating in the air and hounding me to Hades."

Conrad said, "I didn't find a metal briefcase with any papers."

"Of course you wouldn't," Andros said. "Von Berg always liked to say—"

"'It's all in my head,'" Conrad said, completing the sentence. "I know. But what, exactly?"

Andros shrugged. "At least you confirmed he's dead."

"Along with Stavros and the rest of the crew of your boat," Conrad said. "All at the hands of Sir Roman Midas. So now we plot revenge. Isn't that what you Greeks do?"

A cloud formed over Andros's face. "I'm but a humble billionaire, my friend, and barely that. Roman Midas is that many times over, and far more powerful. Especially if he has this weapon you say he took from the *Nausicaa*. Look outside." He walked out to the open balcony.

"I saw it," said Conrad, limping over with the Metaxa and looking out at Garitsa Bay.

To their right the sun was setting behind the old town, its colonnaded houses dating back to the island's days under British rule. To their left the stars were rising above the old Venetian fortifications.

"Look closely," said Andros.

Conrad set the bottle of Metaxa on the balustrade and picked up a pair of Zeiss binoculars. Beyond the stone fortifications of the Old Fort, the superyacht *Midas* was anchored in the bay, with small boats ferrying well-dressed men and barely dressed women to and from shore.

"Looks like he's celebrating his catch of the day," Conrad said. "Any way I can get a closer look?"

"Not a chance. Greek coast guard boats are maintaining a perimeter. And the island is crawling with security."

"Why's that?" Conrad swept the deck with the glasses and noticed the chopper had returned.

Andros said, "The Bilderberg Group is holding their annual conference at the Achillion."

Conrad looked at the ornate palace atop a hill opposite the bay.

"Ironically, it was Baron von Berg's headquarters during the war," Andros told him. "Built by the empress of Austria and later bought by Kaiser Wilhelm II of Bavaria as a winter retreat. It's a fanciful place, with whimsical gardens and statues of Greek gods all over the place. I deflowered many a girl there myself."

"What's the structure next to the palace?"

"The House of the Knights," Andros said. "The kaiser built it to house his battalions. There are nice stables, too, for the kaiser's horses. For all its romance, the Achillion has a long history of military staging. It was strafed by Allied planes in 1943 during the baron's stay and then turned into a hospital after the war. Later, it became a casino featured in a James Bond movie."

"And now?"

"It's a museum, used on occasion as a spectacular backdrop for meetings of the G7 nations, the European Union, and apparently, the Bilderberg Group."

The Bilderbergers. Conrad knew a few of them, including his late father, who had attended a couple of the conferences back in the 1990s when he was acting head of the Pentagon's DARPA research and development agency.

Officially, the Bilderberg Group brought together European and American royalty in the form of heads of state, central banks, and multinational corporations to freely discuss the events of the day away from the glare of the press. Unofficially, conspiracy buffs suspected the Bilderbergers set the world's agenda, orchestrating wars and global financial panics at will to advance some totalitarian one-world government that would arise from the ashes.

"I'm thinking Midas is a member of the Alignment," Conrad told Andros.

Andros looked at Conrad as if he were talking about Atlantis, which in a way he was, as the Alignment considered themselves to be the custodians of the lost civilization's mysteries. "I'll have the doctor check the oxygen in your blood again."

"The Bilderberg Group is the closest real-world equivalent to the Alignment that I know of," Conrad said. "If there are any Alignment members left on the planet, it stands to reason that at least a few of them would be members of the Bilderbergers and use the group as a proxy to advance the Alignment's agenda."

"Just as the Alignment used the Egyptians, Greeks, Romans, Knights Templar, Freemasons, USA, and Third Reich?" Andros said, holding up the half-empty bottle of Metaxa with a knowing smile.

Conrad put down the Zeiss glasses and looked Andros in the eye. "I think I know a way into the party tonight."

Andros frowned. "Who is she?"

"According to Google, she's his latest girlfriend, Mercedes Le Roche."

"Of Le Roche Media Generale?"

Conrad nodded. "Her father," he said. "She used to be my producer on *Ancient Riddles*."

"You're crazy," Andros said. "Put this insane idea out of your head. Get off the island before Midas figures out you survived. Get out while you still can."

"I have to find out what Midas intends to do with that weapon," Conrad said.

"Maybe sell it?"

"He doesn't need the money. He's Midas."

"True," said Andros. "You say this *Flammenschwert* is Greek fire?"

"No, you said it's Greek fire. I said it's a weapon that turns water to fire."

"Greek fire," Andros repeated. "But we Greeks have always called it liquid or artificial fire. We used it to repel the Muslim Arabs at the first and second Sieges of Constantinople in the sixth and seventh centuries. That's how Europe survived Islam for over a thousand years."

"But how did Greek fire work?"

"To this day, nobody really knows," Andros said. "The ingredients and manufacturing process were closely guarded military secrets. The emperor Constantine VII Porphyrogenitus even warned his son in a book to never give away three things to a foreigner: a crown; the hand of a Greek princess; and the secret of liquid fire. All we know is that Greek fire could burn on water and was extremely difficult to extinguish. The sight of it alone was enough to demoralize the enemy. My father always suspected that it was petroleum-based and spiked with an early form of napalm."

"Maybe," Conrad said. "But I think that the petroleum jelly your forefathers used was a crude copy of something far more devastating. Something that used a uranium-like ore that could actually consume water like oxygen, not just burn on its surface. Where did you say Greek fire came from?"

"I didn't," Andros said. "But tradition says it was cooked up by chemists in Constantinople, who inherited the discoveries of the ancient Alexandrian chemical school."

Conrad nodded. "Who inherited the discoveries of the Atlantean school. Only the Alexandrians didn't have access to *Oreichalkos*."

"*Oreichalkos*?" Andros looked mystified.

"The mysterious ore or 'shining metal' mined by the people of Atlantis, according to your ancient philosopher Plato," Conrad said. "Plato called it 'mountain copper.' He described it as a pure, almost supernatural alloy that sparkled like fire. I've seen it before."

"In Antarctica," Andros said with condescension. "Pish. Atlantis was the Greek island of Santorini. I have a hotel there."

"Let's not get into that debate now," Conrad said. "The point is that this technology is older than mere Greek fire. I witnessed what a speck of it can do. I think Midas could fry oceans with it. But which one?"

"My grandfather said Hitler wanted to use it in the Mediterranean," Andros said. "The Nazis wanted to protect

Fortress Europe with a moat of fire and burn the warships of the Allied invasion fleet before they could land. Von Berg, however, wanted to use it to dry up the Mediterranean and proclaim its one million square miles as the new Atlantis."

"Too big, I think, and this is a new century." Conrad shook his head. "Where else in today's world?"

"Where it can do the most damage," said Andros confidently. "The Persian Gulf."

Conrad paused. Here Andros, whose family's tankers brought oil to and from the Persian Gulf, knew what he was talking about. "Go on."

"Midas is in deep with the Russians, and they're running out of production. Best way to boost prices is to cut supply— preferably somebody else's. Especially when the Americans depend on it. What better way to disrupt oil shipments through the Persian Gulf than to set it on fire? Who knows how long it would burn with this weapon?"

"Pretty good."

"I think so," said Andros. "So now you tell your friends at the Pentagon and call it a day."

"Or you get me into the Bilderberg bash."

Andros looked at the imposing Achillion on the hilltop beyond the bay. "My money reaches the Greek police. But the Bilderbergers bring their own security. Even I can't get into that club."

"They publish their guest lists. Maybe I can go as somebody else before they show up. Say hello to Mercedes, get something out of her before Midas knows what's going on."

"And kills you?"

"In front of all the other Bilderbergers? No. I know guys like Midas. Appearances and respectability are paramount. He won't lay a finger on me in front of Europe's rich and powerful."

"No, he'll simply kill you as soon as you step foot out of the palace."

Conrad studied Andros. "What's going on? I say Midas, and your knees start shaking. The guy blows up your boat, kills your crew, and almost kills me, your good friend. Odysseus would have had three arrows in this guy's throat by now."

Andros, in turn, studied him. "You were not always so vengeful. I want to meet the woman who hurt you so badly. So I can introduce her to my rival shipowners in Athens."

Conrad looked out at the lush green esplanade of Corfu town and thought of Serena. "When you find her, let me know. Because she's not taking my calls."

"Forget her," Andros said. "How did you leave things with Mercedes?"

Conrad said nothing.

"I thought so," said Andros. "Why should she tell you anything about Midas or his operations? More important, what makes you think Midas would have told her anything of value that she could pass on to you? My rule is the less a woman knows, the better."

"Which explains the women you go out with," Conrad said. "Look at that boat he named after himself. You know that the richer a man gets, the smarter he thinks he is. Midas is an arrogant bastard, and I'm willing to bet that in his hubris, he's let Mercedes see more about his operations than he's realized."

"Are you willing to bet your life?"

"I did that a long time ago. Midas took his shot this morning. And I'm still here."

"So is he, my friend. And he has an inexhaustible supply of henchmen and money. You are only one man."

Conrad poured some of the brandy into a glass, gave it to Andros, and then held up his bottle in a toast. "What about my buddy the Greek tycoon, who is going to get me into that Bilderberg party tonight?"

5

There were lights and music coming from the Achillion Palace that evening, but no crowds of onlookers, no paparazzi to snap photos as the guests stepped out of their limousines and entered the palace. And the glamour quotient took a distant backseat to the power quotient. Everything was understated and discreet, save for the music: Coldplay live in concert. Actually, it struck Conrad as odd—a bit of contemporary fizz thrown on a very old-world gathering.

Conrad sat in the backseat of his limousine in an Armani tuxedo as Andros played the part of his driver, nudging the sedan forward in the line of black chariots at the main gate where U.S. Marines stood.

Andros, whom Conrad had never seen more nervous, pressed a button to unlock the trunk and then lowered his window for the Marines and spoke in Greek. "His Royal Highness Crown Prince Pavlos."

One of the guards flashed a light at the rear passenger window as Conrad lowered it for them to get a better look at his impression of the Greek royal. The guard matched the name and face to the computerized clipboard while three others with extended mirror plates examined the underside of the sedan and the trunk. Conrad's resemblance to Pavlos was close enough for the Marine, who got the all-clear from the bomb squad and waved the limousine through.

Andros let out a sigh of relief as they rolled down the drive to the entrance of the palace and looked up in the rearview mirror. "This was a bad idea."

"We got through the gate, didn't we?"

"Only because U.S. Marines don't know what Pavlos really looks like up close and in person. His family isn't even of Greek descent. The monarchy was originally imposed on Greece by the Bavarian ancestors of these Bilderbergers. Trust me, the cabinet-level Greeks and *Evzoni* at the entrance will know on sight that you're an impostor."

Conrad knew that Andros was referring to the Greek security detail dead ahead. They were members of Greece's elite ceremonial presidential guard who, besides guarding the Hellenic Parliament and Presidential Mansion in Athens, guarded the reception of foreign dignitaries. Dressed in traditional light infantry uniforms, they wore scarlet garrison caps with long black tassels and red leather clogs with black pompons.

"They're just for show, Andros. Men in kilts."

"And carrying M1 Garand semiautomatic battle rifles with bayonets."

As they pulled up to the columned facade of the palace, Conrad saw four members of the Bilderbergers on the front steps welcoming guests: Her Majesty Queen Beatrice of the Netherlands; His Royal Highness Prince Phillipe of Belgium; Microsoft founder and the world's richest man, William Gates III; and a man Andros said was Greece's minister of finance.

Andros said, "We're cooked."

"Just remember, buddy. You're richer than half of them and better than the other half."

Andros stopped the limousine, and an *Evzoni* opened Conrad's door as another ceremonial guard announced his arrival in English. "Dr. Conrad Yeats, USA."

They knew all along it was me, he thought with a start.

He glanced back at Andros, but the *Evzoni* had already waved off the limousine to make room for the next arrival, leaving Conrad alone to face a smiling Queen Beatrice, who coldly shook his hand.

"So good to meet you, Dr. Yeats. I'm so glad you could come at the last minute as a substitute for Dr. Hawass from Cairo. We're looking forward to hearing your perspectives on archaeology and the geopolitics of the Near East."

"My pleasure." Conrad smoothly shook hands with Prince Phillipe and then Bill Gates. He knew he was a fool to have believed he ever would have slipped anything past these people. They had let him know it and were about to make him an exhibit for public viewing at their little gathering.

"I heard your talk about astronomical alignments and Washington's monuments at the TED conference in Monterey a couple of years ago," Gates told him. "I remember thinking you were either completely nuts or archaeology's equivalent of the world's most dangerous hacker."

Conrad couldn't tell if that was a compliment or indictment as Queen Beatrice indicated he should take her arm and they walked up the three flat marble steps through the main entrance.

Inside the reception hall, arrivals had gathered at the base of an impressive staircase flanked by statues of Zeus and Hera. At the top of the stairs was a grand mural that showed Achilles dragging the dead Hector behind his chariot before the walls of Troy. Conrad hoped it wasn't a prophecy for the evening and that the courtesy of his hostess would be extended to him by the rest. "Why the special treatment, Your Majesty, if I may ask?"

"All of our guests tonight are special, Dr. Yeats."

Conrad watched the crowd move up the grand staircase to the second floor, which opened onto the terrace and gardens outside. The guest list he had seen numbered 150 names—about a hundred from Europe and the rest from North America. Mostly government, finance, and communications types.

One of them, the new publisher of *The Washington Post*, he instantly recognized in front of him. Unfortunately, the tall, thin blonde saw him, too.

"Conrad Yeats, what the hell are you doing here?" she said. "Stepping into your daddy's shoes?"

"Hello, Katharine," he told her. She was wearing her white watch with the rhinestone skull-and-bones face. He had never seen her without it. "You seem to have filled your grandmother's pumps nicely." He watched her move toward the bottom of the grand staircase, where her party was waiting.

"Ah, you know Ms. Weymouth," Queen Beatrice said.

"Just a dance or two in high school," Conrad said. "I thought media was banned from this event."

"Not at all," the queen said. "We have several American and European news organizations represented here. But our participants have agreed not to report on the meeting or to grant interviews to outside press about what transpires. It would defeat the purpose of this forum."

"Which is?" Conrad pressed.

The queen smiled and clasped his hand with both of her own. They were small but firm. "Simply and only to allow world leaders to speak their minds freely."

"I'll do my best," he said, and turned toward the staircase.

"Before you do, your friend and sponsor for tonight would like to speak to you in the kaiser's room," Queen Beatrice said.

"Sponsor?" Conrad repeated, stepping toward the room to the right of the reception hall before the queen tugged his arm.

"That's the chapel. You wouldn't want to go there. Maybe later. The iconography is unparalleled. But the kaiser's room is this way." She gestured to the short hall on the left of the grand staircase. "It was a pleasure meeting you, Dr. Yeats." There was an unnerving finality in her voice.

Conrad bid adieu to the queen, who moved back toward the front steps while he walked down the hall to the kaiser's room and entered the study. There stood a short, barrel-chested penguin of a man in a tuxedo: Marshall Packard, former U.S. secretary of defense and now acting head of its DARPA research and development agency.

"Hell, Yeats, is there any woman alive you don't have a past with?" Packard said.

Packard must have seen his little run-in with Katharine back in the foyer, Conrad realized. "You're violating the Logan Act, Packard, you know that," he said. "You and every American here who discusses anything pertinent to the national security of the United States with foreign powers."

Packard walked behind the kaiser's old desk and made himself comfortable in the leather chair. "Spare me the lecture, Prince Pavlos, and shut the door."

6

Conrad sat down in the kaiser's study and looked at Packard—
"Uncle MP," as Conrad had known him growing up, when he
was his father's old wingman in the air force.

Packard and his father, the onetime Bilderberger, had been
best friends until his father's first ill-fated trip to Antarctica as an
Apollo astronaut on a Mars training mission. Four astronauts made
the mission, but only Griffin Yeats returned alive. The Griffter was
profoundly changed by the mysterious affair, confounding those
who thought they knew him, including his own wife. When the
Griffter introduced four-year-old Conrad to the family as an
adopted son immediately thereafter, the suspicions only grew.

Conrad knew that his adoptive mother had enlisted Packard's
help to get to the bottom of the story. But Packard never did.
Nobody did. Not even Conrad. Not until the Griffter recruited
Conrad for a last-ditch, no-holds-barred military expedition to
Antarctica, where he said he had found a young Conrad frozen
in the ice. That Conrad, in fact, was an Atlantean, and the U.S.

government had the DNA to prove it: Whereas the DNA strand of every indigenous species on earth spiraled to the right, Conrad's spiraled to the left.

Ergo, he was not of this earth.

Conrad almost bought the story, except for the reality that in every other way, his DNA and life were extraordinarily ordinary. Outside of Conrad being of interest to the Alignment types, and the mystery of his alleged Atlantean roots, Uncle Sam really had little use for him beyond his expertise in megalithic monuments, astronomical alignments, and ancient mysteries.

Conrad took another look around the kaiser's study and said, "The Bilderbergers let you do this—go off and have closed-door meetings away from everybody else?"

"Hell, Yeats, that's all we do at these things. Wake up," Packard said, and got down to business. "You need to find out where the hell that *Flammenschwert* went and what the Alignment wants to do with it."

How on earth did Packard know about the *Flammenschwert* or that Midas had it? Conrad wondered. But it took only a second for him to come up with the answer. "So Andros gave me up?"

Packard nodded. "Your boy's family goes way back with us in Greece. He knows who your true friends are, even if you don't."

Conrad said, "Did Andros also tell you he thinks Midas might want to use the *Flammenschwert* to set the Persian Gulf on fire?"

"Hell, I'm worried the Alignment is going to use it in the Caspian Sea and destroy Russia's ability to ship oil," Packard said. "That's twelve trillion dollars' worth of oil right there. Trillion! It's the only thing keeping the collapsed Russian economy going. They lose that, and they won't bother with their Arab proxies. Their tanks will sweep into the Middle East, and we'll respond, and then we've got nuclear Armageddon."

It was a hellish scenario, to be sure. "So you're sure the Alignment is behind Midas?"

"They made him," Packard said. "And since you helped us smash their network in the U.S., they're using the EU as their cover and base of operation. What do you think this bullshit European summit about the fate of Jerusalem next week on Rhodes is all about? You really think European bureaucrats are ever going to agree on anything remotely resembling a 'coordinated, comprehensive peace plan' for the Middle East? It's all a cover. While the French and German presidents preen for peace, the Alignment will be conducting business as usual. They bankrupted the Russians in the nineties. Now they've bankrupted the United States. All that's left for them is to get our armies to knock each other out so they can unite the rest of the world."

Conrad had heard it all before from his father. "How is one man like me going to change any of that?"

"Maybe seeing you tonight will shake Midas up, knowing that you're on to him. Maybe he'll make another mistake."

"Another?"

"You survived your first encounter with him, didn't you? How did you do that?"

"Atlantean blood, remember?"

Packard gave him a funny look, as if he half believed it. *These guys at DARPA,* Conrad thought, *always looking for any way to create the perfect soldier.* "You do realize that I don't work for you anymore, Packard, don't you? I'm under no contract to the Pentagon or anybody else."

"Only your pledge of allegiance to the United States of America, Yeats. And that's worth more to me than all the promises of a U.S. senator. They can be bought, or at least rented. Not you. Now, tell me how you found the *Nausicaa*."

Packard seemed genuinely interested, so Conrad obliged.

"Same way I helped the Greeks here fix April 15, 1178 B.C., as the date of King Odysseus's return from the Trojan War and his slaughter of his wife's many suitors," Conrad said. "I aligned clues about star and sun positions from Homer's ancient Greek epic poem *The Odyssey* and contemporary German and British captain's logs to pinpoint the location of the *Nausicaa* when it sank."

Packard frowned. "The same astrological mumbo-jumbo the Alignment swears by?"

"Not quite," Conrad said. "According to Homer, the goddess Calypso had bidden Odysseus 'to keep the Bear on his left-hand side' until he reached this island of Corfu. I let Ursa Major be my guide."

Packard, satisfied yet again that Conrad was the right man for this job, said, "So you knew the *Flammenschwert* was on board the sub?"

Conrad shook his head. "All I knew was that the sub was returning from Antarctica. I was hoping it was carrying some relic from Atlantis."

"From the pit of hell, for all it matters," Packard said. "This *Flammenschwert* is a game-changer. The world is seventy-five percent water. Whoever rules the waves rules the world. You've got to stop Midas from using this thing or, worse, figuring out how to make more of them."

"How do I do that?"

"Just throw yourself in his face," Packard said. "I told you. Midas thinks you're dead. Maybe the sight of you will prompt him to double-check something with regard to the *Flammenschwert*. Now that we're monitoring him with every conceivable electronic surveillance on sea, land, and sky, we might catch him before it's too late."

"And what do I get?" Conrad demanded. "Just because I can't be bought doesn't mean I wouldn't enjoy some spoils of war."

"You didn't get enough from Uncle Sam for those two Masonic globes you dug up under the monuments in D.C.?"

Packard was referring to Conrad's last adventure with Serena Serghetti, which began at his father's funeral in Arlington Cemetery. Conrad had discovered that his father's tombstone was encoded with Masonic symbols and astrological data. It was yet another riddle wrapped in an enigma for Conrad to solve and Packard to go ballistic over. That tombstone turned out to be the key to a centuries-old warning built in to the very design of Washington, D.C. In the deadly race to decode that warning, Conrad and Serena had discovered two Templar globes of murky origins that America's first president, George Washington, had buried beneath the capital city—one terrestrial and one celestial.

It was the document inside the terrestrial globe that exposed the Alignment's plot to destroy the American republic and ultimately led Serena to steal that globe and take it with her to Rome, leaving the Americans with only one of the Templar globes. Meanwhile, the suspicion at the Pentagon that the globes worked together in some mysterious way probably explained the glare now coming from Packard and his cigar.

Conrad said, "The almighty American dollar isn't what it used to be. I used up my reward from the globes to find the *Nausicaa*. So, again, what do I get?"

"How about answers to all your questions?" Packard said. "Atlantis. Your father. Your birth. Hell, maybe we'll even get to the bottom of those globes."

"I've been to the bottom and back," Conrad said. "I know more about those two globes than anybody."

"Enough to explain how you let one of them slip away to the Vatican with your old girlfriend?" Packard said, lifting his eyebrows and his glass of brandy.

"I'm beginning to hate you as much as I did the Griffter, Packard."

"Then we're all good." Packard got up and ushered him to the door.

Conrad said, "That's it?"

"Text me when you find something," Packard said. "You've got my number. Just say the word and I'll send in the Marines."

"Last time the Marines tried to kill me."

"For all our differences, Yeats, you and I are on the same side. We don't buy any of this 'post–American world' bullshit the One-Worlders are here to propagate. Power and evil abhor a vacuum. We can't let the Alignment fill it."

Packard opened the door, and they walked into the reception hall, where a few late arrivals were making their way upstairs to the terrace.

"Just be yourself," Packard said softly as they started up the grand staircase. "Midas, like you, is a fringe player here—you by virtue of specialized knowledge and him by virtue of his oil billions. He wants to make a good impression on his Alignment masters, whoever they may be. Just seeing you walking around will rob him of that confidence."

They paused at the reception chamber at the top of the steps, in front of the *Triumph of Achilles* fresco. Conrad took a closer look at the gates of Troy in the background and saw a swastika. He knew it had been an ancient symbol of Troy long before the Nazis misappropriated it. But given the circumstances of the evening, it creeped him out just the same.

"What makes you think he's scared of me?" Conrad asked.

"He's not scared of you. He's scared of anybody in the Alignment who sees you here tonight," Packard said. "He'll know that we know he's got the *Flammenschwert* and that we can tie him to whatever happens with this thing. More important, he'll know his friends in the Alignment know it and that you just made him their fall guy."

They were on the second floor, which led outside to a sweeping veranda and the gardens overlooking the bay. This was where the lights and music were coming from, as the women in gowns and men in sleek tuxedos mixed among the life-size statues of Greek gods.

A floating tray with drinks came by. Packard grabbed two and handed one to Conrad. It was a Mount Olympus. Conrad tasted it. Not bad. He nodded and took another sip. They walked outside into the gardens, preparing to separate, and Conrad scanned the faces for Mercedes.

Packard seemed to read his mind. "Looking for her?"

"Gotta play my best hand if Midas is holding all the cards," Conrad said.

"Her Highness is even more of a player than when you last saw her," Packard said. "Never looked better, or more powerful and influential on the world stage."

Conrad knew Mercedes was thin, rich, and French. But "Her Highness" and power and influence never quite fit his picture of her, even when she was his producer playing with her papa's money.

"There's Midas," Packard said, gesturing outside. Conrad couldn't see through the small crowd of Bilderbergers. "He's talking to Her Highness right now."

Conrad wondered which royal princess Packard was snidely referring to. Then two guests parted like the Red Sea to reveal Midas holding court with several admirers around a stunning brunette in a backless black dress.

It was Serena.

7

Serena stood by the bronze statue of the dying Achilles, having traded her parka in the Arctic for a backless Vera Wang. To her left was Roman Midas, the man she had come to meet, representing the Bilderbergers' back channel to Russia. To her right was General Michael Gellar of Israel. Neither man was particularly pleased with the other, as Gellar had essentially accused Midas of providing the uranium for a Russian-built nuclear reactor that Israeli jets had bombed the month before. Now the mullahs in Tehran were threatening to attack Israel through their Palestinian proxies in Gaza and the West Bank.

"Any direct attack on Jerusalem or Tel Aviv will invite a devastating response on Tehran," said Gellar, his hawklike, craggy face looking like it had been cut from the rocks of Masada. "Israel has a right to exist and to defend herself."

Serena eyed Midas as he calmly sipped his vodka and nodded. She had been invited by the Bilderbergers as a Vatican back channel between both of them in hopes of averting the latest Middle

East crisis. But she also wanted to get Midas alone to press him about his mining in the Arctic.

"As you know, General Gellar, I'm a Russian expatriate often at odds with my homeland." Midas affected an odd British accent that Serena thought made him sound like a roadie with Coldplay. "I can vouch from personal experience that these are thugs running Russia now. The government itself is a mafia-like criminal organization. They are looking for any pretext to punish Israel through their Arab allies. If you attack Tehran, you will be handing them that pretext. And then what are you going to do? Nuke Moscow?"

"If our existence as a state is threatened, of course," Gellar said.

"Then Russia attacks America, and we have Armageddon," Midas said. "No more oil. And I'm out of business." He was trying to make a joke out of it, and Gellar grudgingly cracked a half-smile.

Seeing an opening, Serena made her move. "I hear there's always oil in the Arctic," she said, looking at Midas.

"I think the ice would have something to say about that," he said. "But I'd be there in a second if we could drill and ship. It would be the fifth-largest field of oil in the world."

"But what about the damage to the environment?" she asked.

"Moot point," he said. "By the time we ever drilled the Arctic seabed, the ice cap would have already melted completely, and we'd be drilling to fuel the rebuilding of whatever was left after the global floods." As an afterthought, he added: "Global warming is a tragedy."

"Nothing that fossil fuel consumption in the form of oil has anything to do with, I suppose?"

Midas smiled and pushed the conversation back at her. "That medallion," he said, noticing the ancient Roman coin that dangled just above her gown's sequined neckline. "What is it?"

"Oh, it's a coin from the time of Jesus," she said, touching it with her fingers. The medallion designated her status as the head of the Roman Catholic Church's ancient society Dominus Dei, which had started among the Christian slaves in Caesar's household near the end of the first century. It was also a sign, she was convinced, that as head of the Dei, she was one of the Alignment's legendary Council of Thirty. She had begun to be more public in her display of the medallion in an effort to ferret out the faces of others in the council. "My order's tradition says that Jesus held it up when He told His followers to give to God what is God's and to Caesar what is Caesar's."

General Gellar said somewhat dubiously, "That's supposed to be the actual coin?"

"You know some traditions," she said, smiling. "There are enough pieces of the cross for sale at churches in Jerusalem to build Noah's ark."

Gellar nodded wanly.

So did Midas. "Jesus suffered terribly at the hands of the Jews."

Oh God, Serena thought, watching for a sign of outrage on Gellar's face, but there was none. His face was a craggy slab of stone. But then Gellar had fought anti-Semitism from the Nazis, Russians, Europeans, Arabs, and regrettably, even the Church his entire life. He had mastered the art of overlooking the small offenses and forgoing the small battles so long as he won the war. And he had never lost one.

Midas, meanwhile, seemed delighted with the direction the conversation had taken and asked with feigned earnestness, "Tell me, Sister Serghetti, what is Caesar's and what is God's?"

Serena sighed inside, having realized she was foolish to believe Midas would be a gusher of information about his Arctic expeditions. "Basically, Jesus said to pay our taxes but give God our hearts."

"See, this is the problem with the world's monotheistic religions," Midas said quite passionately. "And I include the Russian Orthodox Church. They demand people's hearts. Then they demand people's hands. Then wars start. The world would be better off without religion."

"Wars rarely start over religion," she said diplomatically. "Usually, they start over something two or more parties want."

"Like land?" Midas asked.

"Or oil?" Gellar echoed.

"Yes," said Serena. "They simply use the cloak of religion to disguise their naked ambitions."

"Then let's remove the masks and solve the problem. Like I am doing. By creating more oil."

All at once Midas had made himself and technology the uniter of the world and Serena and her presumably backward faith its divider.

"Technology is no cure for evil, suffering, or death," she reminded Midas. "It is but a tool in the hands of fallen men and women. It cannot redeem the human heart or reconcile the peoples of the earth."

At that the blood drained from Midas's face, as if he had seen a ghost, and the hair on the back of Serena's neck stood on end even before a familiar voice behind her said, "Gee, Sister, how *does* reconciliation happen?"

Slowly, Serena turned to see Conrad Yeats standing before her in an elegant tuxedo, holding a drink in one hand and a cigar in the other. She blinked and stared at him. There was a smile on his lips but hatred in his eyes. She had no idea what he was doing there, only that with Conrad Yeats, there was no telling what he would do, and she was genuinely frightened.

"Dr. Yeats," she faltered. "I didn't know you were a Bilderberger."

"Oh, they'll let anyone join these days," he said, looking at Midas before locking his hazel eyes on her. "So you just forgive and forget?"

There was a pregnant pause, and Serena could feel his gaze on her, along with everybody else's. Except for Midas. His ice-blue eyes, wide with shock, stared at Conrad in disbelief, and in that split second she grasped that Midas had thought Conrad was dead.

"Forgiveness isn't the same as reconciliation," she answered, sounding detached even though her heart was racing faster than her head. "You can forgive someone, like a dead parent, without resuming the relationship. Reconciliation, however, is a two-way street."

"Interesting," said Conrad. "Go on."

"Well," she said, pursing her lips. "The offending party first must show remorse and ask for forgiveness."

"And then?"

"Next the offending party must pay some kind of restitution. After he met Jesus, the tax collector Zacchaeus repaid everybody he ripped off four times over to show his remorse."

"Sounds good to me," Conrad said, puffing on his cigar. "Is that it?"

"No," she said. "Last, the offending party must show a real desire to restore the relationship. That takes trust. And trust takes time."

Conrad nodded and blew a circle of smoke into the air. "What if the offending party doesn't give a rip or return your calls?"

Serena took a deep breath, aware that Midas and Gellar were gone and the circle had broken up, leaving her alone with Conrad, who was ruining everything. "Then you should forgive them but not resume the relationship in hopes of reconciliation."

Conrad looked around and acknowledged that they were speaking privately. "Thanks for clearing that up, Serena. I thought I had just one reason to hate you for the rest of my life after you stole from me and then ditched me in D.C. But you keep giving me more."

"What are you doing here, Conrad?"

"I was going to ask you that very question," he shot back. "I thought Jesus hung out with the poor, the oppressed, the sick. Not the rich and powerful."

"It's not like that, Conrad."

"Then enlighten me, please."

She told him. "I think Midas is helping the Russians mine the Arctic. I want to stop them."

"Interesting," Conrad said. "Midas tried to kill me this morning."

"Really?" she said, hiding her concern. That meant both Midas and Conrad knew something she didn't. It had to be something terrible to bring together two such extreme men in her life. "I hope he has a ticket. The line seems to get longer each year."

"Lucky you," he said, looking over her shoulder. "It looks like my number is up."

At that moment Sir Midas's girlfriend, Mercedes, waved and headed toward them with a smile. "Conrad!" she called out.

Serena whispered into Conrad's ear: "Squeeze her for information. She might confess some things to you that she wouldn't to a nun."

He looked at her with contempt. "You want me to sleep with her because your vows keep you from sleeping with Midas?"

"Something like that," she said. "You were going to anyway, weren't you?"

The look in his eyes told her that she had hurt him, and she hated herself for it. But it was better than him harboring any hope for her, as much as she was dying to be with him. Because there wasn't any hope as long as the Alignment lived.

"You're just a cast-iron bitch with a crucifix, aren't you?" he said.

The words pierced Serena's heart as Mercedes arrived, but she forced a smile.

"Professor Yeats!" Mercedes said, giving him two air kisses on each cheek.

Serena said innocently, "I forgot you two worked together."

"Truth be told, Professor Yeats worked for me until he didn't work out at all," Mercedes said, and gave her a wicked wink. "Sister Serghetti, if you'll excuse us, I'm going to have to take the professor away and spread him around."

Serena wanted to reach out and grab Conrad's arm to keep him from walking away with the woman. But she could only nod politely as she stood by herself next to the statue of the dying Achilles.

8

Conrad knew that he had come tonight to see Mercedes, whom he reluctantly followed past security down some stone steps into the lower gardens. But the sight of Serena had so thoroughly thrown him that Mercedes could have stripped off her snug gown and invited him to skinny-dip with her in the sea and he still would have passed on the opportunity in order to get back to Serena. Or get back *at* her. He wasn't sure.

Mercedes, meanwhile, looked incredibly if artificially well sculpted in her silver halter dress. Her forehead and facial features, however, seemed a bit too tight when she turned to him in the dim light of the lower gardens. Sure they were at last alone, she slapped him across the face.

"You bastard!" she hissed. "You stranded me in Nazca with a stolen artifact and a dozen Peruvian soldiers."

He rubbed his stinging cheek with his hand. "You got out okay, didn't you?"

"And how do you think I managed that?" she said, tearing up. "You think those pigs cared who my father was?"

It dawned on him what must have happened, the favors she was forced to offer to get out while he was off in Antarctica with Serena. He couldn't tell her he'd had no choice, because in hindsight, he had. It hadn't been necessary to leave her on that plateau. He could have insisted that the U.S. military take her and drop her off somewhere safe before proceeding. And he hadn't.

Conrad said, "You told me later that all was forgiven and forgotten."

Her eyes turned into black slits, the moonlight giving them an otherworldly glow. "Because I had to," she said. "I was hoping you'd come back. But you didn't, did you?"

Conrad, realizing that Mercedes's feelings toward him were the same as his own toward Serena, felt horrible and gave her his full attention. "I'm here now."

"No, you came to see *her*," Mercedes said, referring to Serena.

"Actually, I came to see your boyfriend," he said, surprised that he was actually telling her the truth.

She believed him, it seemed, and said nothing for a couple of minutes as they walked down more steps to the beach. There was a tiny Greek fishing village there, with some modest homes behind whitewashed walls. She removed her stiletto sandals, and they walked along the sand to the old stone bridge jutting out into the water.

"This is the kaiser's pier," she said. "He used it to go back and forth from his yacht."

"Like Midas?"

Her slits for eyes softened into a worried look. "What's your business with Roman?"

"He stole something that belonged to me."

She forced a smile. "I doubt that."

"That he stole something?" Conrad asked.

"That whatever he stole belonged to you. What was it, Conrad? Some Greek statue at the bottom of the sea?"

"Something important enough for Midas to blow up my boat and kill my crew over." He was as serious as he had ever let her see him.

She paused. "And so you decided to come back for more?"

"Did you hear me, Mercedes? Your boyfriend killed people today. You don't seem surprised. And that surprises *me*. What are you doing with a monster like Midas?"

"All men are animals." Her eyes narrowed back into slits. "But Roman is an adult, Conrad, not a child like you. He understands power and money and politics in a way you never could."

"All I understand, Mercedes, is that Midas seems to have moved on from oil to arms."

Mercedes sniffed. "I don't believe you. Midas doesn't need anything in this world. He's as rich as, well, Midas. He doesn't have to steal anything. He can buy it."

Conrad said, "Then tell me what he's buying these days besides megayachts and art."

A shadow passed across her face, betraying the fact that, yes, Midas had bought something interesting lately. "You haven't changed, Conrad," she said. "You're looking for links that don't exist. The great conspiracy is that there are no conspiracies. Everybody is out for himself. Life is a big black hole. There is no meaning."

"Your existentialism used to have some romance, Mercedes. What happened?"

Her phone beeped, and she glanced at a text message and shook her head. It must have been from Midas, Conrad thought. "Romance is dead," she told him. "And so are you if you go after Roman."

She took his hand to lead him back to the party when two security men came down the steps, talking softly into their radios. "You fool, it's too late," Mercedes said, sounding genuinely alarmed.

Conrad looked over his shoulder past the kaiser's stone pier. A light in the distance grew closer, and soon a dinghy emerged from the mist around nearby Mouse Island, like a boat from the River Styx, with a large, muscular colossus of a man standing at the prow.

"You've got to be kidding me." Conrad had started to turn back to Mercedes when he felt the stab of a needle in his neck and blacked out.

9

A bucket of freezing water brought Conrad to life. He blinked his eyes open. He seemed to be inside the submersible launch bay of the superyacht *Midas*. The hatch was open wide over the surface of the water. Moonlight reflecting from the sands beneath the yacht bounced around the hold. He was sitting in a chair, his feet bound together at the ankles and his hands tied behind him to the back of the chair.

"What is the four-digit code, Professor?" said a voice with a thick Russian accent.

Conrad looked up to see a bodybuilder type towering over him. Behind him stood two security men and a giant basin of water. They were leaning against a double-domed deep-flight Falcon submarine. Midas must have used the Falcon to transport the *Flammenschwert* from the *Nausicaa* to the yacht, Conrad thought.

"I don't know about any four-digit code," Conrad said, trying to quickly make sense of his predicament. He should be dead.

Maybe Midas hadn't found everything he was looking for in the *Nausicaa* and was hoping Conrad had. "But I'm sure glad you told me about it."

The Russian held up an electric shock baton. Conrad recognized it as the type favored by the Chinese police in torturing Falun Gong practitioners. "Maybe this will jog your memory," the Russian said.

Conrad shivered as the picture came into focus: He was drenched in water in order to intensify the three hundred thousand volts of electricity this thug was about to apply to him.

"I know you," Conrad told him, and he realized where he had seen the face. "You're that ex–KGB guy turned fitness guru with the kettle ball infomercial."

The Russian paused, seemingly pleased at the recognition. "It is true. I am Vadim."

"Too bad your website sucks. Bet your online sales of those Vadimin supplements do, too. Is this your day job, or do you have another one at some health spa?"

Vadim cocked his thick head. Conrad was clearly getting inside it, and the Russian didn't like it. He plunged the electric baton into the fresh harpoon wound in Conrad's leg.

Conrad gritted his teeth as the voltage shot up his thigh and throughout his body. For a second he thought his head would explode. When the wave of devastating pain finally passed, he dropped his head and saw that the baton had reopened his harpoon wound, which oozed blood.

"Utter a sound, Dr. Yeats, and I'll shove this baton into your mouth and shock you with a thousand root canals at once until you black out."

Conrad could smell his own burned flesh. It would take weeks for it to fully heal. Not that Vadim was intending for him to see that day. The Russian pressed the wound with the baton until a shard of harpoon protruded up through the blood. Conrad moaned in agony.

"Go easy on the lad, sport," one of the other guards said in a British accent. "Midas wants to get the code out of him before he dies."

So the other two were Brits, Conrad thought. Private security. For all Conrad knew, Midas also employed former Navy SEALs and American mercenaries in his private global army. Who said capitalism was dead?

"Shut up, Davies," Vadim told the Brit sternly while he trained his eyes on Conrad. "Von Berg's code," he repeated. His breath was foul. "Four digits. Like your hand after I cut off your thumb." He pulled out a cigar cutter. "Or maybe I'll cut off something else. Now tell me where the code is."

"Of course!" Conrad cried out. "It's all in my head!" He started to laugh uncontrollably, despite the pain. It was crazy, but by rephrasing his demand for the code in terms of "where" instead of "what," Vadim had triggered an epiphany for Conrad. Now Conrad understood why nobody had found a metal brief-case containing secret codes inside the sunken sub. The paranoid Baron of the Black Order never carried secret papers in a brief-case or on his person on land, sea, or air. Von Berg knew he'd be dead if anybody found them. So he kept the code in his head, literally. And that head was back in Conrad's room at the Andros Palace Hotel.

Vadim and the Brits glanced at each other. "You find this funny, Dr. Yeats?"

Conrad nodded. "Let me guess. This code Midas wants. You don't know what it's for, do you?"

Vadim said, "You will tell us?"

"Hell, no. But Midas is going to assume I did. And then you guys are dead."

Vadim's nostrils flared. "What are you talking about?"

"I know what Midas stole from the sub this morning. Don't you?"

It was clear from Vadim's expression that he did not.

"Oops," Conrad said. "Maybe you're not as tight with the boss as you thought."

Vadim's eyes dilated at the truth of Conrad's words. Indeed, Vadim seemed to be reconsidering his relationship with Midas.

"What's more likely?" Conrad asked, relentless. "That Midas is going to kill you because I got away? Or because you know what he stole from the sub and where it might be?"

"Kill him," said Davies. "But get out of him what he knows."

Conrad looked at Vadim. "The only way to pull it off is like this: You have to make Midas believe you killed me before I said anything. But how is he going to believe that and keep you around? You have to make it look like I killed one of the Brits while trying to escape and that the other one came in and shot me."

"How stupid do you think I am, Dr. Yeats?" Vadim pulled out a 9mm Rook pistol of the type favored by Russian special forces and put it to Conrad's forehead.

"Quite stupid, actually," Conrad said.

Vadim shook his head, swung his arm to the side, and shot Davies in the head. Davies fell to the floor.

"Bloody hell!" screamed the other Brit, and pointed his Browning pistol at Vadim. "You killed him!"

Vadim shot the other Brit, and Conrad watched him crumple on top of his fallen comrade. Conrad, still in agony from the shock baton, kept laughing as Vadim put his gun away.

Vadim picked up the shock baton and glared at him. "You will now reveal the four-digit code, Professor Yeats."

"Look!" Conrad was staring at the bloody black hole in his thigh. "Look at what you did."

With a smile, Vadim bent over to take a closer look.

Conrad kneed him with both legs to the face, driving the protruding harpoon shard into Vadim's eye. The Russian snapped his head back with a howl. Then Conrad used his bound feet to sweep the leg of the table with the basin of water, sending it crashing to the floor.

As Vadim staggered back, his boot slipped on the water, and he lost his grip on the shock baton. Conrad watched the baton fall to the floor and lifted his feet as a blue wave of electrical light rippled across the water, electrocuting Vadim like an X-ray.

When Vadim came to a few minutes later, the yacht's "abandon ship" alarms were blaring, and Conrad was gone. In his place was a gray-green brick of C4 explosive with a timer and Davies's cut-off middle finger sticking up on top.

The display on the timer was down to one minute and twenty-three seconds. *"Chyort voz'mi!"* Vadim cursed, and scrambled topside to discover that the skeleton crew had left with the shuttle tender, leaving him no choice but to jump overboard and swim for his life.

10

Serena was alarmed to see Mercedes come up from the lower gardens alone and immediately went out on the terrace to search for Conrad, to no avail. She did, however, find Packard by the stone balustrade with a drink in his hand.

"What are you doing, Mr. Secretary?" she demanded. "Where's Conrad?"

"Elvis has apparently left the building," Packard told her. "And Midas doesn't look too happy."

Serena followed his gesture toward the statue of Apollo, where Midas seemed to be having a low-key but sharp exchange with Mercedes.

"Guess Midas just figured out that you're not the only woman here tonight who has a past with Yeats," said Packard, taking another sip of his drink. "Now, what's up in the Arctic?"

Serena tore her eyes away from Midas and looked at Packard. "Midas is prepping to mine it for the Russians."

"You sure it's for the Russians?"

"Who else?" Serena asked.

Packard finished his drink. "Your friends in the Alignment."

Serena looked out over the bay, where she could see Midas's yacht sparkling on the waters. "I have no friends in the Alignment," she told him. "Only enemies."

"But thanks to your corrupt holy order, Dominus Dei, of which you are now the head, you are by definition one of the Thirty."

Serena took a deep breath. "And as soon as I figure out who the rest are, I'll let you know."

"You were talking to one of them."

"Midas?" she said. "How do you know he's not just working for them?"

"He knows too much," Packard said. "More than you, it seems. Financial records in London show that Midas's trading firm went long on oil and gold futures this morning. If he really expected the Russians to succeed in the Arctic, he'd be shorting oil on the expectation that a new supply would depress global prices. Instead, he's betting on a spike in prices."

"Interesting," Serena said. "Midas must be anticipating a disruption in oil production."

"Or some other event that would shoot up the price of oil. Maybe a major war."

"So he knows something we don't," she said, and then she realized something. "And so does Conrad."

"You should fix that."

"Listen, I told you about Midas's operations in the Arctic. Have you given any thought to returning that celestial globe to the Vatican?"

"Have you given any thought to returning the terrestrial globe you stole?" Packard shot back.

"We've been over this, Mr. Secretary. The Masons inherited them from the Knights Templar."

"Who in turn stole them from Solomon's Temple," said Packard. "So maybe we give them both back to the Israelis."

Serena sighed. "Along with another American weapons system, perhaps? That will help the situation in the Middle East."

"The only thing you can do to help the Middle East and the rest of the world is to give us the real names and faces of the Alignment's so-called Thirty," Packard said. "Before Yeats finds out you're one of them. Get busy. Here comes Midas." Packard walked away as Midas approached her.

"Was that the former U.S. secretary of defense?" Midas asked Serena innocently enough.

"Yes," she said. "Confessing all his country's sins. Do you have any confessions you want to share?"

"Actually, I was looking for Dr. Yeats. He seems to have disappeared."

There was a feigned playfulness in Midas's voice, but his eyes were hard. He was lying, she realized. Midas knew exactly where Conrad was.

"So has Mercedes," she said, and his smile vanished.

Midas said, "She had a headache. Dr. Yeats upset her."

"He has that effect on women," Serena said when her Vertu phone rang with the song "He's a Tramp" from Disney's old *Lady and the Tramp* cartoon. "Speak of the devil."

Midas cocked his head and narrowed his eyes with suspicion as she took the call.

Conrad's voice, breathless, filled her ear: "Have Benito pick me up in front of the Andros Palace Hotel in Corfu town in two hours. I need to hitch a ride with you on your jet."

"We're all here for three more days," she said, eyeing Midas.

"I don't think these Bilderbergers like talking to police," Conrad said. "They're all going to scram before they give any statements about what they saw."

"I'm not sure I understand."

"Take a look out at the *Midas* in the bay. She sure looks like a beauty out there on the water, all lit up."

Serena glanced at Midas, then out at the water. "Yes, she does."

Suddenly, the superyacht blew up into the night sky like fireworks, drawing gasps from the crowd on the terrace. An explosion like thunder rolled over the bay. Midas crushed his glass in his fist. Wine and blood dribbled through his fingers. Serena watched his face twist into a monstrous mask of rage as the glowing debris of his beloved ship rained down upon the waters.

11

A panic-stricken Andros was waiting for Conrad at the service entrance behind his hotel. "You blew up the *Midas*!"

"Where's the head of Baron von Berg?" Conrad demanded as they hurried through the kitchen.

"In your bag in the room's closet. I couldn't stand the sight of it. Nor of you now, my friend."

They were standing at the service elevator. Conrad, his tuxedo soaked, realized he had been dripping a trail of water behind them. Two Greeks with mops were furiously following in their footsteps. The hotel's owner, Conrad had heard, was a stickler for cleanliness.

"All you have to do is smuggle me off the island, Andros," Conrad said, and pressed the elevator button again.

"I'm working on it, but the police and coast guard are everywhere now." Andros shook his head. "You've really done it this time, Conrad. Mercedes is up in your room."

"What?" Conrad stopped cold as the light dinged and the elevator doors opened.

"She showed up just before you did." Andros nudged him inside. "You have to see her."

"But Midas sent her."

"Of course," said Andros. "Which is why you have to see her. He must hope to get something out of you."

"You mean the ice pick she'll plant in my back?"

"Maybe, but you might get something out of her. Meanwhile, give her some disinformation to take back to Midas. I'll have your ride off the island ready in twenty minutes."

"This could take longer than twenty minutes," Conrad said, knowing that Mercedes wasn't going to divulge important information to him just because he'd asked.

"Nonsense," said Andros, all business. "It took you only half as long with my cousin Katrina, and that's how you found me."

The doors closed, and Conrad rode the elevator to the top floor, where he walked down a short hallway to his room. Two security guards with earpieces were posted on either side. Conrad fished inside his pocket for his key card and realized he had lost it. That was probably how Midas and Mercedes had learned where he was staying.

"*Parakalo?*" Conrad asked a guard in Greek. "Please?"

The guard opened the door for him, and he walked inside. The lights were dimmed, and the smooth jazz of Nina Simone was playing over the stereo speakers.

Mercedes was standing outside on the balcony, just beyond the rippling drapes, a glass of wine in her hand. It must have been at least her third glass, because the bottle in the ice bucket was almost empty. Her head tilted when the door clicked shut behind him.

He walked up beside her. Out in the bay, the Greek coast guard had spotlights over the wreckage of the *Midas*. He could hear the garble of megaphones in the wind. "What do you think we're going to do here tonight, Mercedes?"

She turned to him with her crystal-blue eyes, which were dried out and bloodshot. He had never seen her cry, and it appeared he never would. "You have no idea who Midas is and who his people are, Conrad."

"Oh, you mean the Alignment," he said, taking the glass from her hand and finishing the wine, aware of her stare. "I know. They're a sinister centuries-old group who count themselves as the heirs to the knowledge and power of Atlantis. They use the stars to wage their endless campaign to manipulate governments, armies, financial markets, and the course of human events. Their goal is a one-world government in effect if not name. In other words, ultimate power. Based on what they've already accomplished with the worldwide depression and de facto one-world central bank, I'd say they're halfway there."

She didn't appreciate his glibness. Her eyes turned into slits. "Then you know we're both dead."

"Speak for yourself, Mercedes. But I think you're better off telling Midas that your charms of old worked, that we slept together and you know I'm taking a plane out of here in the morning to Paris, where your well-heeled family can help me. Better yet, you're on that plane with me. Only we're landing in Dubai, where my well-heeled friends can help you."

She said nothing for a minute, her eyes drifting to the wine bottle and seeing it was nearly empty. "I am not a whore, Conrad."

"I didn't say you were."

"You were the one willing to prostitute yourself for the sake of your useless digs around the world," she went on. "You were willing to make love to me just to get my father to fund your stupid TV show. And you ditched me in Peru with those animals."

"I have no excuse, Mercedes. I'm sorry. And I know there's nothing I can do to make it up to you."

She put her hand on his chest and gently pressed him back toward the bedroom. "Oh, but there is, Professor," she said, regressing to her producer's "role" as his beautiful graduate assistant when he was still dividing his teaching duties between the University of California at Los Angeles and the University of Arizona.

"Two wrongs don't make a right," he told her as she began to unbutton his shirt.

"Like you and Serena? You two don't add up. You never did and never will."

"What about you and Midas?"

"He's rich and powerful. Powerful in a way you'll never understand."

"Because he's a player for the Alignment?"

"Maybe." She kissed him on the cheek.

"What did he do to make their ranks? Or did they make him?"

"I don't know," she said, moving to his ear. "Hard to tell with most of them."

"What does Midas do for the Alignment?"

"Mining and money," she said, clearly displeased to be discussing business. "His mining operations help governments, and his futures trading firm in London evens things out in the financial markets. As per Alignment protocols, his top traders use astrological charts to hedge their bets. That's why Midas Minerals & Mining is also called M3."

"And I thought M3 was my old BMW sports car."

"M3 is a constellation," she said.

Conrad perked up. "A constellation?"

"Canes Venatici. It's thought to represent the two dog stars of—"

"The herdsman in the sky, Boötes," Conrad said, unable to forget from his last run-in with the Alignment that the White House in Washington, D.C., was by design aligned to the alpha star of Boötes, Arcturus. Boötes was mythologically connected to the constellation Ursa Major—the Great Bear—from which Russia took its own identity. "I hate all this Alignment bullshit." He hated it because it reminded him of how ignorant he was of just how deep the celestial machinations and symbols of the Alignment went, and how far back—eons and eons. It was like encountering an alien race. And Mercedes had knowingly thrown in her lot with them.

It was all very suspicious, and he was already past the twenty minutes Andros had given him.

Conrad gently folded his hands around hers. "Where is Midas taking the *Flammenschwert*?" he asked.

Her face was blank. "*Flammenschwert?*"

"It was the name of a hammerhead torpedo the Nazis developed using some advanced technology. It means 'Sword of Fire.'"

"I know what *Flammenschwert* means," she told him curtly. "My German always was better than yours. But I know nothing of any *Flammenschwert.*"

"Oh, you think Midas took his yacht out to deeper waters this morning simply for pleasure cruising?"

"Yes," she said, clearly irritated.

"So you never wondered why he outfitted his superyacht with a submersible and a chopper pad?"

"I always assumed it was for effect." She sniffed.

He looked into her eyes—wide open now—and felt she was telling him the truth. It made sense to him that she'd projected onto Midas some of the foibles of her past and the men who were part of it, including him.

"Know anything about the four-digit code Midas is looking for?" he asked.

The slits returned. "How do you know about it? Did she tell you?"

By "she," Conrad figured Mercedes meant Serena. "No," he told her, letting her read his own eyes. "You think it's for the *Flammenschwert?*"

"No," she said, and Conrad could see the light go out of her eyes as she sat on the bed. "It's for a safe deposit box."

"And Midas owns it?"

"No," she said. "You asked me if Midas has purchased anything lately. He owns the bank in Bern that holds the box. Gilbert et Clie."

Conrad wasn't sure he understood. "So he bought the bank to get to the box? That's one way to raid a tomb. What's in the box?"

"Nobody knows. It belonged to some Bavarian prince. Ludwig von Berg."

"Baron von Berg the Nazi?" He had to force himself to keep his eyes fixed on hers, to not let them drift to the closet where Andros had stashed the bag with the skull.

"Yes, yes," Mercedes said. "It's an older type of box with a chemical lining. It has a four-digit alphabet code. One wrong letter in the combination, and the contents of the box are destroyed. There's only one chance to open the box. And Midas needs whatever is inside within the next seven days."

"Seven days?" Conrad asked, realizing the world was going to be introduced to the *Flammenschwert* in short order.

"Seven days," she repeated. "Good Friday, two days before Easter."

"Is that significant to the Alignment?" Conrad asked. "Is there a connection?"

"I don't know," she said. "It's significant to me because Easter is the only Sunday of the year that I've ever gone to church."

"You're a real saint," he said. "But what's Midas doing spending three of his precious seven days with the Bilderbergers?"

"The Achillion was Baron von Berg's headquarters during the war," Mercedes said. "Midas had hoped to find some clues the baron might have left behind."

"He didn't leave any," Conrad said. "He kept everything in his head."

"I know. So I can't help you. And you can't help me."

Conrad, holding her hand, got down on one knee. "I told you, Mercedes. Come with me to Dubai and we'll figure it out."

She shook her head. "You know more than anybody else that there's no escaping the Alignment."

"Then come with me to Dubai," he told her. "Andros has the jet waiting. We'll be there in under three hours."

"And then what, Conrad?" She challenged him with her eyes. "We live happily ever after? Or you ditch me again?"

"I'm not going to ditch you, Mercedes."

"But you're going to leave me."

"I'm not going to stay with you, if that's what you mean."

"Then what's the point?"

"I want to help you," he said.

She looked at him with disdain, seemingly surprised by his naïveté. "I don't care how much money your crazy Arab friends have, Conrad. Nobody runs away from Midas. He'll find you. And your friends will give you up in a heartbeat for less than the price of this." She held up her hand to show the glittering diamond bracelet dangling from her wrist. From the looks of it, Conrad calculated that it had cost Midas at least $1 million. A trinket for him, a handcuff for her.

"I'll give you thirty minutes before I call Midas," she said with finality. "Enough time to make it to the airport and take off."

"And you?" Conrad asked as he stood up and walked to the closet.

"I'll tell him you were asking about the *Flammenschwert* and that I offered to put you up at my apartment in Paris. Old Pierre will let you in."

Conrad pulled out his bag and slung it over his shoulder. "What happens when I don't show?"

She shrugged. "We'll all know you lied. Like you always do."

12

Vadim was parked across from the service entrance of the Andros Palace in the dark, making his calls while he waited for Mercedes to emerge. He set his 9mm Rook on the passenger seat next to his copy of *The Four-Hour Workweek*.

Despite his boasting to Yeats, his Vadimin vitamin supplements were not selling as well as he had hoped. So while Yeats was undoubtedly making love to Sir Midas's French *blyad*, Vadim was on his cell phone making calls on behalf of the collection agency Midas owned in Bangalore to shake down money from customers behind on their credit card payments. He took perverse pleasure in squeezing money from the debt-ridden pockets of Americans and their knowledge that foreigners were doing it.

A figure stepped outside the hotel—Yeats, from the looks of him at a distance—and climbed into a black BMW 7 series sedan. Vadim started his car and caught a glimpse of his own face in the mirror. He saw the patch over his eye and cursed. The BMW drove off.

Vadim pulled out and had started to follow it around front when Mercedes emerged from the hotel's main entrance and walked toward him. He stopped and let her climb in the back.

"You were supposed to kill him," Vadim said as he drove off after the BMW.

"So were you," she said sharply. "He's going to the airstrip."

Vadim looked up in the mirror. "And from there?"

"Athens, Dubai, God knows where," she said. "I invited him to my place in Paris."

Very clever, Vadim thought. She had guessed that Vadim's orders were to kill her as soon as she killed Yeats. This way she had hoped to keep herself alive a while longer. But if Yeats got off the island alive, Vadim's orders were to kill Mercedes instantly and make it appear that Yeats had done it. The time of death would be vital for the Greek coroner's report.

The car with Yeats stopped ahead. Two police cars were blocking its path. Vadim slowed down and watched as the police made the passenger step out of the limousine for inspection. Only it wasn't Yeats. It was a slightly younger man—Chris Andros III, the Greek billionaire.

"What is the meaning of this?" Andros asked.

"*Signomi, Kyrios* Andros. We thought you were somebody else."

"Obviously, you're mistaken. What do you want?"

"Where are you going?"

"My jet. I have business in Athens, as you know."

"Our apologies," the police officer said.

Vadim didn't bother to watch Andros get back in his sedan; he had already reversed course and was driving back on a small dirt road. In the mirror, he could see Mercedes getting nervous.

"Where are you taking me?" she said.

Vadim pulled to a stop and looked over his shoulder at her. She was scared. She should be. "Did you lift Dr. Yeats's fingerprints like Sir Midas requested?"

"Yes, off a bottle of wine," she said, and handed him a white card with Dr. Yeats's fingerprints trapped on clear tape. "What is Conrad supposed to have done now?"

"Killed you with this gun," said Vadim as he leveled his Rook over the seat and shot her twice in the chest.

13

At the Corfu airport, the twin turbofan Honeywell engines of Serena's private Learjet 45 hummed while she ran through the preflight checklist with the pilot and copilot. Both had more hours in the air than she did, and both were former Swiss special forces airmen she trusted with her life, let alone a short fifty-minute hop to Rome. But she hadn't heard from Conrad yet, and this took her mind off him for the moment.

"Check the thrust reverters again," she said when she was finished. "I thought I heard something."

She went back into the passenger cabin, sat down in a recliner seat, and glanced outside her window at all the private Gulfstreams lined up to go. The scene was the same in Davos, Sun Valley, San Francisco, and everywhere else she had ever seen the billionaire set meet. Her own Learjet was a hand-me-down from an American patron who had moved on to an even more expensive pair of wings. All the planes on the tarmac this morning resembled a line of luxury cars exiting a parking lot after a

sporting event. Only this event—the sixtieth Bilderberg meeting—
had barely begun.

Now it was over.

Conrad was right: Every European and American master of
the universe was scrambling to escape the island before the police
and paparazzi could question him or her. The weekend conference
was in shambles, along with Sir Roman Midas's great superyacht,
which no doubt was going to fire the imaginations of Bilderberg
conspiracy theorists for years.

The truth, of course, was much simpler: Conrad Yeats.

Wherever he was.

The Vertu phone she was clutching in her hand vibrated. It was
Marshall Packard, calling from his private jet on the other side of
the runway. "You're losing your grip, girl," he barked. "Where the
hell is Yeats?"

"I don't know," she said, alarmed. "What's going on?"

"Turn on the goddamn TV."

Serena clicked a small remote to turn on the cabin's TV. The
local Greek channel came up first, but she didn't have to be fluent
in Greek to understand the picture of Mercedes Le Roche—dead
at thirty-two. She had been found at a local beach, shot in the
chest.

"Oh, no," Serena said under her breath. "Conrad."

As if on cue, Conrad's picture showed up. He was the prime
suspect in her death. His fingerprints had been found all over the
murder weapon—a 9mm Rook.

"Conrad prefers a Glock," Serena said quickly. "He didn't kill
Mercedes."

"No, he was either killed with her or is about to join her," Packard said sharply before he hung up.

Serena looked out her window to see Benito pulling up in the car, then talking to the Greek police as he stepped out. They were conducting a plane-to-plane search for Conrad Yeats. They were paying particular attention to her plane, no doubt courtesy of Midas. They needn't have worried.

Benito boarded the plane, shut the door, and sat down in the aisle across from her as the engines grew to a dull roar. They were cleared for takeoff. She held her breath while Benito solemnly fastened his seat belt and looked at her with sad, soulful eyes.

"I'm sorry to tell you, *signorina,* that once again Dr. Yeats has fooled us all."

She breathed a sigh of relief. "Thank God."

14

Conrad looked at himself in the broken mirror of his private compartment as the Czech-built diesel locomotive hauled the train clickety-clack across the Albanian countryside. He had boarded the train as a swarthy Mediterranean workman and would disembark as a Central European businessman in a dark Brooks Brothers suit, with lighter hair, goatee, and spectacles.

That was assuming the train reached the end of the line. The Mother Teresa international airport in Tirana was only an hour away, but they were going less than thirty-five miles an hour.

Conrad had escaped Corfu and crossed the Adriatic to the southern coast of Albania in under thirty minutes, all thanks to the hydrofoil Andros had provided, along with fake passports, a bag of disguises, and two untraced smartphones, a BlackBerry and an iPhone, each operating on a separate network carrier. From the beach at Durrës, he had made it to the local train station, where he first saw the news about Mercedes and his picture on all the news websites on his iPhone.

Goddamn bastards, he thought as he gave himself a final once-over in the small mirror.

He was thinking of Midas and the Alignment, Packard and the U.S., and even Serena and the Church. Everybody, in the end, was in bed with each other when they weren't killing each other. Also, it bothered him to no end to see that he had better cell phone reception in Albania than he had back in the States: He had just received his electronic boarding pass from Swissair in his bogus identity's e-mail inbox.

He put away his makeup and glared at the only other passenger in the private compartment of this secondhand railroad car: Baron von Berg. Sitting on a torn seat, the skull taunted him with its jagged grin and the secrets it once possessed.

It's all in my head.

Conrad pulled out the Glock he kept tucked inside his back waistband. Aiming the butt of the pistol like a hammer over the skull, he brought it down on the silver plate, smashing the skull to pieces. He looked at the fragments of bone scattered around the silver plate on the table.

Nothing. The skull was indeed empty.

Then he picked up the silver plate. He turned it over and held his breath. There was a glint of small engraving in the silver.

"Von Berg, you crazy bastard," Conrad said as he took a closer look at the engraving.

It was a string of eight characters—four numbers followed by four letters: 1740 ARES.

There it was: 1740 had to be the number of Baron von Berg's safe deposit box in what was now Midas's Swiss bank. And ARES had to be the combination.

This was the four-digit code Midas was looking for.

He had it and Midas didn't.

But with the Alignment, there was always more, he knew. Nothing could be taken for granted.

Ares was the name of the ancient Greek god of war. The astral projection was the constellation Aries, the first sign of the zodiac. The planet Mars, with the Roman name of the same Greek god, had entered the sign of Aries two weeks ago on March 20, the spring equinox.

A coincidence?

Not for these Alignment bastards. Every day and date had some sort of bizarre meaning for them, if for nobody else.

There was probably an astrological connection that could throw light on the baron's 1943 plans for the *Flammenschwert* and Midas's plans for it in the new millennium.

Mercedes had said something about seven more days. That would be one week from today—Good Friday for Christians around the world, according to the Gregorian calendar. There would be a full moon that night, followed the next day by the Jewish Passover and the day after that by Christian Easter.

Beyond those dates, Conrad saw nothing else of astrological or astronomical significance on the calendar while the zodiac was fixed in Aries.

Seven days.

Whatever was going to happen with the *Flammenschwert* was going to happen then. And the religious significance of the dates only further confirmed the magnitude of the Alignment's plot, whatever it was.

The train's wheels made a high-pitched screech, and Conrad looked out to see a sheer cliff as the train hugged a mountain above the Adriatic. He took the opportunity to toss the silver plate out the window and scatter the remains of the skull over the waters. Not quite a proper burial for the Baron of the Black Order, but it would have to do.

By the time the train pulled into the station in Tirana, he was all packed up and ready to step off into his new identity. He scanned the platform for any security and grabbed a cab to the Mother Teresa airport.

An hour later, he leaned back in his seat as the Swissair plane lifted off the runway and banked toward Zurich. The seat belt sign blinked off a few minutes later, and flight attendants took drink orders. He ordered two Bloody Marys, one for Serena and one for Mercedes, painfully aware that he'd just had a very close call and that this was the last free pass he'd enjoy on the journey before him.

PART TWO

Baku

15

A darkened military car carrying one American and three Azerbaijani special forces commandos rolled through the city's old town toward the harbor before dawn.

Riding shotgun in the front passenger seat with an AG36 40mm grenade launcher across her lap was the American, a knife-thin black woman in her early thirties with short hair and sharp features. Her name was Wanda Randolph, and her mission was to intercept and secure a mysterious shipment that had landed at Heydar Aliyev International Airport, sixteen miles east of Baku. The airport's advanced Antworks computer software and scanner system had tagged and tracked the crate through the cargo terminal's state-of-the-art X-rays and radiation detectors to an awaiting van. The van had taken the crate to a warehouse on the Caspian, where it was waiting to be loaded onto an oil tanker.

The operation was code-named *Feuerlöscher*—German for "fire extinguisher."

The commando raid was to be carried out jointly by American and Azerbaijani special operations forces and locals. The mission had been mounted rapidly overnight on orders from the Central Intelligence Agency and the Defense Department when the location of the crate had been confirmed. Another dozen American commandos in a specially equipped Black Hawk were ready to swoop in if the team got pinned in a gun battle.

Wanda glanced up from the glowing GPS map that General Packard had sent to her handheld computer. The ancient walls of the Palace of the Shirvanshahs, the Maiden Tower, and the Juma Mosque rose up on either side of the narrow, twisting alley. Then the car cleared the maze of buildings, and the pitch-black Caspian Sea spread out before them, marked by the lights along the waterfront.

The Caspian was called a sea because, at 143,244 square miles, it was the world's largest lake, smack between Russia to the north and Iran to the south. Azerbaijan occupied the western shores, and tonight it felt as if the city of Baku stood at the edge of the world, a world that itself was teetering on the brink of a bottomless abyss.

"Take a left," she told the driver, a young macho gun named Omar.

"Yes, ma'am," Omar said in a bogus Oklahoma accent, eliciting muffled chuckles from the other two in back. All three had been trained in a cross-cultural Oklahoma National Guard training program with the U.S. Army and loved to play the American cowboy in the new Wild West here on the Caspian. But none had ever been ordered to listen to a woman, let alone one of color, and they resisted. The election of America's first black president, it turned out, wasn't going to change human nature or much of anything else in this world.

They turned onto Neftchilar Avenue and drove along the waterfront boulevard and marina. They quickly passed the state oil company and government house and, a few minutes later, were surrounded by the oil derricks and pumps of the east harbor.

At last she could make out the warehouse where the van with the crate containing the *Flammenschwert* was parked. She directed Omar to park at the adjoining oil terminal, then led them to a communal outhouse.

"Why have we stopped?" Omar said once they were inside and could talk quietly. He was breathing through his mouth because of the stench. "The warehouse is the other way."

"Sorry to disappoint you, Omar. But we can't go storming in like Rambo if there's any chance they've got some kind of nuclear device. We've got to take them by surprise." She unfolded her schematics of the sewer tunnels. "No radios," she instructed them. "We stick to light signals until we get to the warehouse, and then it's hand motions."

She looked up and locked eyes with each man as she spoke. She wanted to make sure they understood her perfectly.

Standing around in their black-on-black Texas Ranger base-ball caps, flak jackets, and special night-vision hazmat masks, the Azerbaijanis could pass for one of her old U.S. special forces teams. Wanda had gotten her start years earlier in Tora Bora and Baghdad, crawling through caves and bunkers and sewers ahead of American troops in search of al-Qaeda terrorist leader Osama bin Laden and, later, Iraqi dictator Saddam Hussein. Bomb-sniffing dogs had the noses to find explosives, but they didn't have the eyes or sense to look out for trip wires in the dark. So she was always the first one in. Later on she was recruited by the U.S. Capitol Police to establish a special recon and tactics squad, or RATS, to police and protect the miles of utility tunnels beneath the U.S. Capitol complex. "Queen Rat," they called her.

But Omar and his friends weren't at that level of professionalism yet. They were inexperienced in these kinds of operations, a political necessity for a "joint" American-Azerbaijani mission that was anything but. Tonight was a baptism by fire.

"This outhouse is connected to an ancient sewer that pipes into the modern one under the warehouse," she told them, pointing to the map. "We come up from beneath, use a camera to get a read-out, and then we hit them and secure the package."

She double-checked to make sure they had properly inserted the translucent magazines of their laser-sighted G36 machine guns. Their short-stroke gas systems enabled them to fire tens of thousands of rounds without cleaning, perfect for these guys. Then she proceeded to unbolt one of the rusty metal latrines from the concrete floor to reveal a big black hole.

Omar could only stare in horror as the mission she described on the schematic finally sank in. "This is a shithole!"

"That's what we Americans do, Omar. Climb through shit-holes all over the world to make it a safer place."

He shook his head in horror. "I cannot fit through that," he said with disdain. "My shoulders are too wide."

Which was true. A man's shoulders were often the limiting factor in this kind of work. For women, it was their hips; Wanda's were unusually slim. But while women could do little to narrow their pelvis, men had other options.

"Dang, Omar, you're right. Here, let me take a look," she said, and with an open palm made a powerful thrust to Omar's right shoulder. The blow dislocated his shoulder, and it dropped like a hanging outlaw in an old western. "Oops."

"You American bitch!" he cried. "You broke it!"

"I can fix it when we get out. But now you can squeeze in."

He opened his mouth to protest, but she gave him her angry-black-woman death stare until he calmed down. She then strapped her grenade launcher to her back, slipped on her mask, pushed aside the metal latrine, and dropped into the sewer.

It was cool and dark in the tunnel as she crawled on all fours through the river of filth and oil. One spark and they'd all burn to a crisp. It had been in a crumbling, asbestos-lined tunnel much like this one that she had first met and shot at Conrad Yeats. Yeats had been America's most-wanted man at the time. Now he was Europe's most-wanted man. Or he would be once news got out that he had blown up billionaire Roman Midas's megayacht and allegedly killed his French media scion girlfriend.

But General Packard had been proved right again: The sight of Yeats had been enough for Midas to double-check his operations and, in so doing, betray the location of the package she was after. The breakthrough had come when the tail sign of Midas's twin-engine G650 was caught over the Black Sea by the cockpit cameras of an unmanned Israeli G550 AWACS, or airborne early warning aircraft, equipped with the Israeli Phalcon radar system and satellite data links. The Israeli plane's onboard SIGINT equipment then captured and analyzed the pilot's electronic transmissions and traced them to a cell phone owned by Roman Midas.

Wanda followed the schematics to reach the end point under the warehouse. She snaked a fiber-optic camera through the grating of a drain and got a visual on the van sitting on the loading dock.

She signaled her team, and they took up positions beneath the grating. It was the size of a manhole cover back in the States. She poked it with the barrel of her AG36 and found it heavy but movable. She slid it slowly across the concrete floor and climbed out into the warehouse, followed by Omar and his buddies, who looked like rats on a drowning ship coming up for air.

Omar's arm was dragging. Wanda put her slimy hand over his mask and, staring into his wide eyes, hammered his shoulder back into place while she muffled his cry. They moved out quietly, awaiting her signal.

The van sat there in the dark with a driver behind the wheel while the sound of a motorboat grew louder. She looked through her nightscope and saw two flashes from the sea. The van replied by flashing its headlights twice. A minute later, a boat pulled up, and four black-clad men jumped out.

The van door slid open to reveal the driver and a crate. The driver stepped out to meet the men but then dropped to the ground as one of the seamen slashed a knife across his throat. The killer silently kicked the body into the water and walked to the crate and hauled it over. He flashed a sign. Now four men appeared. He cracked open the box and lit a cigarette.

Wanda squeezed the trigger, and Mr. Marlboro crumpled to the ground. By the time his companions saw, it was too late. A hail of bullets from the Azerbaijanis rained down on them and riddled the van with bullets.

"Stand down!" she shouted, and ran over to the crate while the others jogged after her. "It's a miracle you didn't blow us all up!"

She broke open the crate to find a dead dolphin on a block of dry ice. The stench was rank. She heard something behind her and turned to see one of her boys puking out his last meal: lula kebab with walnuts. She was about to call this red herring in to Packard, but he had already seen everything from her head camera and was cursing loudly into her ear.

She ripped off her earpiece and looked at Omar, who had helped himself to the Marlboro of the dead man and was smiling. "You see something funny here, Omar?"

Omar started laughing.

She repeated, "I asked if you see something funny here."

"You," Omar said, pointing the cigarette at her as he blew a perfect ring of smoke. "You have shit on your face!"

16

Midas couldn't help but note all the sale items on display in the storefront windows along an empty Bond Street in the early morning as Vadim drove the Bentley toward the world-wide headquarters of Midas Minerals & Mining. The golden glass tower was designed to look like a stack of gold coins overlooking the River Thames. But the global financial depression had come into full force by the time it was finished, making it a symbol of excess from an earlier gilded age.

His beloved megayacht was another symbol of that era, and the *Times* of London had taken the liberty of printing two pictures—before and after—on the front page by the time Midas had landed after his unplanned early departure from Corfu two hours ago. Below the fold was a smaller story about the murder of Mercedes.

That goddamn American. Yeats left me no choice.

Midas hated losses, and to take them at the hands of a two-bit pirate like Conrad Yeats was doubly humiliating. He hated feeling like he was cornered.

Now his BlackBerry smartphone was vibrating in a manner that told him Sorath was calling. Midas reached into the long trench coat he had put on upon landing—the air in London being considerably more chilly than on the tropical island of Corfu—and answered the phone.

The disembodied voice of the grandmaster of the Knights of the Alignment was chillier still, and wasted no time making accusations.

"I warned you not to attempt to kill Yeats, Midaslovich. You betrayed yourself to the Americans, and now you are brazen enough to think you can bargain with us."

Sorath sounded particularly displeased, but maybe it was just because there was a deeper bass level than usual in the harmonics of the voice scrambler that disguised his identity. For the past year Midas had tried to find a voiceprint match, all in vain. Only a face-to-face at the Rhodes summit next week would reveal the grandmaster's true identity and whether or not Midas already knew the man.

"I've done no such thing," Midas replied coolly.

"Then why, after all we've done for you, did you feel the need for extra insurance?" the voice said. "I'm speaking of the American strike inside Baku an hour ago."

"They found nothing," Midas said. "And neither did the man you had in place to relieve me of the *Flammenschwert*."

"What have you done with it?" Sorath demanded.

Midas smiled. Sorath wasn't God, and it was pleasant to hear him admit as much. The grandmaster of the Knights of the Alignment wasn't omnipotent, and he certainly wasn't omniscient, or he would have known from the start that Midas never would have allowed himself to become expendable to anybody.

Which was why Midas had offloaded the *Flammenschwert* from the *Midas* to his second submersible while making everybody think he had sent it off by chopper. That submarine was completely undetectable as it made its way underwater until the proper time for it to surface. Meanwhile, Midas was untouchable.

"My orders were to bring the *Flammenschwert* to Uriel," he said. "And so I shall. Nothing has changed."

"Yeats changed things. Mercedes Le Roche is dead, and you're being tracked by the Americans and Scotland Yard."

Midas turned to look out the rear window and saw the unmarked police car in the distance. Two of them had been following him ever since his private jet had landed at Heathrow.

"KGB, CIA, MI5, it matters little to me," Midas said. "I've dealt with them all, and I'm happy to provide misdirection by simply going about my business as usual. I'm here in London for the weekend, then to Paris for Mercedes's funeral, and then off to Rhodes as scheduled."

There was a pause on the other end. "Did you find the code to Baron von Berg's box?"

Midas said nothing as Vadim pulled the Bentley up to the main entrance of the Midas Center.

"You know the requirements for full membership in the Thirty, Midaslovich," Sorath said. "I'd hate to have you miss our little private gathering during the Rhodes summit."

Midas heard the telltale series of beeps signaling that Sorath had hung up and their scrambled transmission was over.

Midas rode a glass elevator up from the sparkling six-story atrium of the hotel, shops, and offices into the tower of private condominiums. Few Britons knew or cared that the award-winning building, his firm's trading in precious metals, his widely publicized purchases at art auctions at Sotheby's, and even his knighthood by the queen all had been part of the Alignment's strategic branding effort to paint him as something other than another former Russian oil oligarch. Even if that was how Sorath and the Alignment preferred to treat him.

Midas walked into his bedroom and into the second of his vast walk-in wardrobe rooms. On the racks hung dozens of Savile Row suits like the one he was wearing, and on the walls hung several million-dollar paintings he had purchased at Sotheby's and later found too ugly to hang anywhere else.

He sat on one of the overstuffed chairs and unlaced his shoes, pulled off his socks, and removed every strip of clothing. He then stood before the row of mirrors and examined his sculpted physique.

He still had a six-pack abdomen, although he'd once boasted an eight-pack when he went fishing with Putin a few years back. The former Russian president always liked to remove his shirt in the great outdoors for the cameras, so the people would know their leader was virile and strong. Putin had not liked it when Midas removed his own shirt and showed him up, and Midas was never invited fishing again.

He saw his right hand trembling slightly in the mirror and closed it into a quiet fist. He opened it, and the fingers began to tremble again. With a sigh, he pushed a button, and the mirror slid open like a door to reveal a stone chamber with a glowing spa in the center. The Tank, as he called it, was his only real weakness and altar to the mysticism of the Alignment. But the reality of his long-term exposure to cyanide as a child and the resulting neurological condition had forced him to seek a cure regardless of its source. Without a cure, he would eventually suffer the same fate as the divers he had gassed in the decompression chamber aboard the *Midas*.

Lining the floor, walls, and ceiling of the chamber were bluestones from the same quarries used by the ancients centuries ago to erect the monument of Stonehenge, Britain's darkest mystery. Most archaeologists believed Stonehenge was an astronomical observatory of some kind, erected around 2500 B.C. But others long had suspected the bluestones were far older and that Stonehenge was a place of healing for pilgrims from all across Europe.

Bluestones, it seemed, were prized for their healing properties. And it was none other than Conrad Yeats, ironically, who had used the stars to help a team of British archaeologists from Bournemouth University pinpoint the exact location in Wales from where Stonehenge's massive bluestones were quarried—Carn Menyn Mountain in the Preseli Hills of Pembrokeshire.

As for the spa in the center of the bluestone floor, Midas's mistress in London, Natalia, had filled it with kabbalah water. Her friend the American pop star Madonna had sworn by it when she purchased a flat in the tower.

Kabbalistic wisdom, Natalia had told him with a straight face, taught that water was God's medium for the creation of the world and was the essence of all life on earth. In the beginning, God's spirit moved across the face of "the deep" that was pure, positive, and healing energy. But then the "negativity" of humanity—she refused to use the word "sin"—by the time of Noah's Flood had changed the nature of water into a destructive force of floods, tsunamis, and the like. Kabbalists believed that water could be returned to its primordial state of good by infusing it with ancient blessings and meditations.

That was how kabbalah water came to fill Midas's bluestone spa, with all its miraculous powers of restoration and healing.

The Alignment, of course, had a different term for this kind of allegedly metastasized water: Tears of Atlantis. The Knights of the Alignment consumed it as a special-label drinking water courtesy of the Hellenic Bottling Company, which also distributed Coca-Cola across Europe and the Middle East.

Midas could only smile as he pictured a small team of kabbalists, all sworn to secrecy, chanting away in some obscure distillation room at the bottling plant.

On one crazy level, it made sense to him that water was a conductor of energy and that the quality of the water he took into his body impacted the information being transmitted to his nervous system. At the very least, it gave his London mistress something to do with her friend Madonna besides run off and spend his money on yet another money-losing retail store for her hideous fashion lines.

He stepped down and settled into the warm amethyst-colored waters of the spa. He reclined in the sculptured stone seat built into the bluestone basin and glided his hand past a sensor. Music piped in, and an overhead door of solid bluestone slowly slid over him and locked into place. The glass screen across the entire back of the door enabled him to surf the Internet, watch any television channel, and monitor his businesses around the world. But for now he put on his favorite screen saver of soothing light, closed his eyes, and laid his head back until only his eyes, nose, and mouth broke the surface of the water.

Kabbalah water. Bluestones with healing powers. Such articles of faith were nonsense to Midas. But these immersion experiences in the tank seemed to have arrested the progression of the neurological condition brought on by his long-term exposure to cyanide. Slowly, it was taking over his body and would eventually kill him. He had to stop it. He would do anything to live.

Even cave to the mysticism of the Alignment.

17

ROME

Later that morning, the events of Corfu still fresh in her psyche, Serena stared through the tinted window of her limo at the obelisk in St. Peter's Square as Benito drove through the gates of Vatican City on the eve of Palm Sunday and Easter week celebrations.

As she checked her Vertu phone, she couldn't shake the memory of Conrad the night before, the hatred in his eyes. He had left her no message. Nor any clue as to his whereabouts. But she did have an Evite to the funeral of Mercedes Le Roche in Paris on Monday, along with a personal e-mail from Papa Le Roche himself, the Rupert Murdoch of French media, begging her as a friend of the family to attend.

"You have enough worries without him, *signorina,*" said Benito, looking up in the mirror, reading her thoughts. "He can take care of himself. You must fix your eyes on Rhodes."

"I know, Benito," she said. "But it's different this time. I feel it."

"It's always different, *signorina*. Every time we pass through these gates. And so it is always the same."

True, she thought as they curved along a winding drive and arrived at the entrance of the governorate. Eight years ago the pope had met her in a secret office here and given her an antediluvian map along with a holy mission to uncover ancient ruins two miles beneath the ice in Antarctica. Four years later, in that very office, the diabolical Cardinal Tucci had revealed to her the truth behind the Church's supersecret order Dominus Dei. Then he had jumped out a window to his death. Now the office was hers.

The Swiss Guards in their crimson uniforms snapped to attention as Serena walked inside. She passed a hive of offices along an obscure hallway to an old service elevator.

In normal times the elevator would take her up to the fifth floor and her suite of offices, which officially interceded on behalf of persecuted Christians in politically hostile countries and unofficially administered the work of Dominus Dei. But these were anything except normal days. She pressed her thumb to a button with no markings that scanned her biometrics, and the elevator descended to the catacombs beneath Vatican City.

She felt like a prisoner in her own castle and remembered the words of Jesus in the Book of Revelation: "Look, I'm standing at the door and knocking. If anyone listens to my voice and opens the door, I'll come in and we'll eat together." He had been talking about the door of the human heart, but He just as easily could have been talking about the Church. After all, God had called St. Paul to go beyond his Jewish world in order to bring the message of redemption through faith in Jesus Christ to the Greeks and, ultimately, to Caesar in Rome.

Perhaps it was "out there" that God had been calling her all along, beyond the walls of the Church. She had cloistered herself here, she had told herself, to protect Conrad and the Church and the world. But maybe she was doing more harm than good. After all, Jesus was more likely to be found beyond the domes and spires and walls of Vatican City, with the people He called "the least of these." Not with the rich and powerful or religious, whom she had found to be as poor and weak and worldly in spirit as anybody.

Yet here she was, locked inside the holy gates of Rome.

Serena stepped off the elevator onto a secret floor deep beneath the governorate. She walked down a long subterranean tunnel to a heavy ornate door behind which the Dei kept priceless artifacts collected from around the world and across the ages. If it were her choice, she would have returned most of them to museums in their cultures of origin. But it was not.

Indeed, her choices of late seemed to be more limited than ever.

Waiting for her inside the dimly lit chamber was a young monk from the Dei and the two otherworldly copper globes that he was guarding. Brother Lorenzo was one of the Vatican's top authenticators of antiques and therefore one of its top forgers of art. He knelt before Serena and kissed her ring with the Dominus Dei insignia.

"Your Eminence," he said. "Welcome back."

Serena, extremely uncomfortable, looked down at the top of the monk's bowed head and withdrew her hand from his clasp. The Church didn't allow female priests, let alone female cardinals. But as the head of Dominus Dei, she was automatically considered a "secret cardinal" appointed by the pope. A secret cardinal to hide the secrets of the Church. Not that the current pontiff, as traditional as they came, would ever acknowledge her as such. But to her amazement, the Vatican did secretly acknowledge the rank of her office, if not the officeholder. Her frighteningly eager underlings, hoping to gain the office for themselves someday, took every advantage to freely address her as such.

"Thank you, Brother Lorenzo. You can call me Sister Serghetti."

Lorenzo rose to his feet, but his covetous gaze was fixed on the medallion dangling from her neck. "Yes, Sister Serghetti."

As she had explained to Midas, legend had it that the ancient Roman coin in the center of the medallion was the very Tribute Penny Jesus had held up when He told His followers that they should "render unto Caesar what is Caesar's and unto God what is God's." It had been passed down through the ages from one leader of the Dei to the next. Some argued that it represented power greater than the papacy. Which no doubt explained Lorenzo's disturbing fascination with it.

Serena broke Lorenzo's trance with an order: "The globes, Lorenzo."

"This way, Sister Serghetti."

She followed Lorenzo to the small alcove showcasing the globes, one displaying the surface of the earth, the other display-

ing the heavens. Each sphere was eighteen inches in diameter and resembled the works of the Dutch master cartographer Willem Bleau's studio in the sixteenth century. But these had been constructed thousands of years earlier, although her attempts to date them proved inconclusive.

Both Church and Templar tradition suggested the globes once rested atop the twin columns that stood at the entrance of King Solomon's Temple. But the Knights Templar believed the globes themselves were crafted far earlier. While Noah was building his ark, other children of Lamech were engraving the globes with the lost knowledge of Atlantis and the antediluvian world so that knowledge would survive the coming destruction of the Flood. The globes, the Templars believed, contained or pointed to some pre-Genesis revelation.

The only legend that Serena had been able to authenticate with any degree of certainty, however, was that the globes had been unearthed beneath the Temple Mount in Jerusalem by the Knights Templar.

Centuries later, the Masons took them to the New World and buried them under what would become Washington, D.C. That was where they rested until the twenty-first century, when Conrad Yeats dug them up before the Alignment could.

The globes apparently worked together like some kind of astronomical clock in a manner that Serena had yet to figure out. But she was positive it involved a secret code or alignment between a constellation on the celestial globe and a landmark on the terrestrial globe. After all, Conrad's knowledge that Washington, D.C., was aligned to the constellation of Virgo had led him to the location of the globes. So it made sense to Serena that the alignment of the globes themselves led to an even greater revelation—a revelation that for centuries had eluded the Church, the Knights Templar, the Masons, the Americans, and everybody else.

Everybody, that is, except the Alignment, which had ordered her to deliver the Templar globes next week to the meeting of the Council of Thirty on the island of Rhodes, all under the guise of the European summit on the fate of Jerusalem.

Serena ran her hand over the smooth contours of the continents on the terrestrial globe, marveling at its three-dimensional, holographic look. "Now tell me what you discovered with the terrestrial globe," she said to Lorenzo.

"The terrestrial sphere is full of hidden gear wheels that, in turn, drive the most unique surface dials I've ever seen on an ancient astronomical clock."

"What dials?"

"The northern and southern hemispheres of the terrestrial globe are really dials," he said. "Inside the mechanism are gear trains that drive the dials. The gear trains are driven by a crank that is inserted into a tiny hole at the bottom in Antarctica."

She looked closely at the tiny hole in the ancient landmass of East Antarctica. It was in the shape of a pentagon. "How could I have missed it?"

"It is rather small." Lorenzo pulled out a tiny S-lever that he had reproduced, inserted it into the hole, and began to crank it. "It works like a keylock, moving the hidden gears within the shell."

To Serena's amazement, the surface of the terrestrial globe began to change before her eyes like some kind of high-definition animation. The continents didn't move, but the contours within them shimmered for a moment and locked into place. "What happened?" she demanded.

"This," said Lorenzo, removing the lever and inserting a penlight into the hole. Three pinpricks of light burst forth from the terrestrial globe in the locations of Antarctica, Washington, D.C., and Jerusalem.

"It's a triangle," Serena said decisively. "Just like the U.S. Capitol, the White House, and the Washington Monument. Those monuments lined up with the constellations of Boötes, Leo, and Virgo. Likewise, these three capital cities from the terrestrial globe should line up with three constellations on the celestial globe."

"The problem, of course, is that the real celestial globe is still with the Americans," Lorenzo reminded her. "And you've never seen it with your own eyes, only the terrestrial globe you stole from Dr. Yeats. He's the only person alive who has seen both globes, which puts us at a terrible disadvantage. The faux globe I've created over here is merely my attempt to mirror in astral terms the mapping I've gleaned from the terrestrial globe."

All true, unfortunately, Serena thought. Her plan had been to procure the genuine celestial globe from Marshall Packard in exchange for her intelligence on Russian mining operations in the Arctic. But that plan had gone up in flames on Corfu. So she had been forced to resort to Plan B.

"I did the best I could," Lorenzo explained weakly as he showed her the two globes side by side—the forged celestial globe and the genuine terrestrial globe.

"Oh, dear," she said, unable to hide her disappointment. The celestial knockoff looked markedly inferior next to the terrestrial globe.

"Our metallurgists, meanwhile, tell me that they've never seen anything like the copper-bronze ore from which the original globes were cast," Lorenzo said. "What you see is their best attempt to match its appearance."

Serena tried to suppress her alarm. They had but seventy-two hours to fix this disaster, and there were no second chances with the Alignment. "Give me the penlight, Lorenzo."

Lorenzo handed it to her, and she inserted it in the tiny hole at the bottom of the forged celestial globe. Three pinpricks of light appeared in the constellations of Orion, Virgo, and Aries: the buckle star Alnilam on Orion's Belt, the alpha star Spica in Virgo, and the brightest star, Alpha Arietis, in Aries.

"I selected Orion and Virgo based on what you told me about Antarctica and D.C. And I selected Aries for Jerusalem because Aries is the cosmic Lamb and Jerusalem is where the globes are said to originate."

"I can accept that. Now we have to hope the Alignment will accept the forgery as the real thing." She looked carefully at Lorenzo's creation. "If we can't bring our celestial globe up to the quality of the terrestrial globe, then maybe we can degrade the look of the terrestrial globe without damaging it. Maybe dull it down with a coat of something or other."

"It still won't hold up to Alignment scrutiny," Lorenzo said.

"Of course it won't," she snapped. "I just need it to pass a quick visual and let the Alignment test the terrestrial globe first."

"How are you going to get them to do that?"

She didn't have an answer yet, and she didn't want to indulge Lorenzo's anxiety with an attempt. The best she could do was fool the Alignment long enough for her to unmask the rest of the Thirty. The American Twelve had been unmasked by Conrad. The remaining eighteen members were European, including her as the head of the Dei. That left seventeen more to unmask at the council meeting on Rhodes.

"That's my problem, Lorenzo. Yours is to prepare these globes for their journey to Rhodes. You need to start working with the Greeks to get the globes through security at the EU summit. We're also going to need two custom shell crates with insulated cavities for transport."

Lorenzo nodded and left without another word, closing the heavy ornate oak door behind him.

18

It was a five-hour drive from Zurich Airport to the chic ski village of Gstaad. The A1 autobahn took Conrad and his rented BMW through the Swiss capital of Bern. He fought the temptation to drive by Midas's bank containing the secret safe deposit box of Baron von Berg and instead turned onto the A6 to Thun, where he exited on Route 11 for Gstaad.

He had one shot to break into that bank, and the only man who could help him was hopefully still holed up in these Alps.

Conrad arrived just after the runs had closed and the five-star restaurants, bars, and discos were filling up with the fashionably rich of Europe, the Americas, and the Middle East. He parked his car several blocks from Sultan's Palace and walked the rest of the way. He had exchanged plates with another BMW at a restaurant stop outside Zurich while the owner was inside eating. All the same, it would be nice to have the car buried under snow by morning.

Sultan's Palace was the grande dame of Gstaad, a multi-spired castle combining the intimacy of Aspen's Little Nell with the majesty of St. Mortiz's Badrutt's Palace. Besides its breathtaking views of mountains and crystalline lakes, it boasted five restaurants, three bars, a world-renowned spa, and the members-only Sultan's Club, infamous across the Alps for its live music performances, dancing, and endless revelry with no curfew. It was, in other words, the very embodiment of its owner, Abdil Zawas, the man Conrad had come to see.

Conrad walked a red "flying carpet" across a frozen moat and through a regal gate into the palace's elegant lobby. At the front desk, he asked for the general manager. While he waited, he looked around at the guests sharing drinks by the fireplaces.

The hotel certainly attracted an unusual quotient of celebrities and royals, he thought, starting with Abdil himself. His mother's side of the family traced itself to Egypt's deposed monarchy, the house of Mohamed Ali Pasha. His father's side of the family, however, had made Abdil first cousin to the late, great Egyptian air force colonel Ali Zawas, whose death Abdil at one time blamed on Conrad.

Come to think of it, Conrad recalled, at some point or other Abdil may have issued a fatwa against him. He hoped Abdil had remembered to rescind it after Conrad helped him out with the design of the Atlantis Palm Dubai resort and theme park. It would be just like Abdil to have forgotten that all was forgiven.

"*Guten Abend, herr,*" said a man's voice.

Conrad turned to see the hotel's middle-aged general manager looking him up and down. Apparently, the German approved of the ski outfit Conrad had swiped from an unsuspecting doppelgänger back in baggage claim in Zurich.

"Good evening," Conrad replied in English. "I'm here to see Abdil."

The manager's eyes narrowed. "You have an appointment?"

"I don't need one."

The German regarded him dubiously. "And who may I say is calling, *herr*?"

"The *herr* who did this," Conrad said, and slid the front page of the Berlin daily *Die Welt* across the desk. He had picked it up in Zurich and now tapped his finger on the photos of the *Midas*.

The manager frowned but took the page and said, "A moment, please." He disappeared into a back office. Conrad could hear the dial tone and clacking of a fax machine. This was followed by a conversation in German that was too quiet for him to make out.

The hotel manager emerged again, all smiles. "This way, *herr*," he said, and escorted Conrad across the lobby to the hotel's three elevators. "His Highness will see you now."

"How high is my friend Abdil these days?" Conrad said.

The German was not amused. "The Sultan's Palace rests at an altitude of only thirty-two hundred feet, quite low for the Alps and just right for an undisturbed night's sleep. But our slopes are over nine thousand feet. So we always remind our guests to drink plenty of water to stay hydrated."

Conrad said, "I'm sure there will be plenty to drink with Abdil."

The doors of the middle elevator opened to reveal two security types, definitely Middle Eastern, with earpieces and bulging shoulder holsters under their expensive-looking suits.

Conrad glanced at the hotel manager, who gestured to the elevator. "*Guten Abend, herr.*"

Conrad stepped inside. The doors closed, and one of the security guards slid a special card key into a slot to unlock access to the hotel's penthouse floor. He pushed a series of buttons in combination, and the elevator began its ascent to the very top of the palace.

The doors opened to reveal a spectacular two-story stone-and-glass penthouse. The last rays of sunset streamed in through the atrium windows between rock walls with waterfalls. The room's size dwarfed that of the hotel lobby, and the clusters of furniture sets, fireplaces, and marble spas were populated with women in various stages of undress.

A voice called brightly from above: "Ah, the enemy of my enemy!"

"Is your friend," Conrad said, glancing up to see Abdil, with the wild mane of a black stallion, waving from the top of the sweeping marble staircase.

The big Egyptian was in his trademark royal bathrobe and boxers, and as he descended the steps with much fanfare, Conrad could see the pearl handle of a Colt pistol tucked inside his waistband. Abdil fancied himself Lawrence of Arabia without the horses and dung, preferring to plot his next moves from the comforts of his pleasure palaces across the globe. He preferred Switzerland to Egypt in order to better tap the global financial markets—and to avoid extradition for his off-balance-sheet activities.

"Welcome, my friend," Abdil said and gave Conrad a kiss on each cheek. "Come to my private dining room."

A woman appeared on either side and helped Conrad off with his coat. He followed Abdil to a dining room with a spread of food that resembled the brunch buffet at the Four Seasons in Amman, Jordan.

"Do you know what it's like to build the world's greatest yacht only to have a Russian thug build one but a meter longer?" Abdil said, taking a seat. "I might as well have been circumcised by the Jews."

"Well, you're the . . . longest on the seas once more," Conrad said. He was tempted to add that it all would be for naught if Abdil kept walking around with a Colt jostling in his boxers. "So I was hoping you could do me a favor."

"Favor?" Abdil's eyes lit up. Conrad liked that Abdil never resented doing favors; he always trusted his negotiating skills to extract something more valuable in return. "Please tell me how I can help my friend."

"Midas owns something you were once interested in," Conrad said. "A bank in Bern called Gilbert et Clie."

Abdil nodded. "The bank of Nazis, Arabs, and other assorted terrorists," he recited sarcastically. "Slander, I tell you."

For several years, Abdil had been on the U.S. global terrorist watch list at the behest of the Saudis, who claimed that Abdil posed a greater threat to the House of Saud than Osama bin Laden. Conrad knew Abdil was no Muslim fanatic, much less a terrorist. Why blow yourself up for seventy-two virgins when you already had them at your beck and call?

Abdil's "big idea" had been to flood the Middle East with mobile phones. While the ayatollahs blew hot air in mosques and on state television, Arab boys and girls prohibited from even acknowledging the opposite sex in public could now text each other behind the backs of their parents. Abdil believed mobile networks would effectively multiply the "disruptive force" of American popular culture—the more profane and nonsensical, the better—and break the centuries-old lock of Islam's paternalistic society, upending the despots in the region with a true democratic revolution. Abdil was indeed an Arab radical of a different kind.

What had soured Abdil and the Americans on each other was the CIA's interference in his operations with cellular network carriers. The Americans wanted to operate or at least control the networks to better monitor voice and text conversations. Abdil couldn't get them to understand that this wasn't at all the point and that they were behaving no better than the despots they hoped to depose. The funds at the heart of Abdil's great Arabian youth mobilization network, held at the bank of Gilbert et Clie in Bern, were frozen. What kind of world was it, Abdil had complained, where you could own your own bank and yet not tap your own money?

Conrad looked at the giant lobster tail that had just been placed before him and asked, "Why did you let Midas buy the bank?"

"Because I saw no upside," Abdil said as he tore into his own lobster. "The rules of Swiss banking and international terrorism are such that if there were any advantage to one party owning the bank itself, then no other parties would hold their deposits there. No fun at all for me. But you obviously think Midas has some advantage?"

"There's a safe deposit box inside the bank that he wants," Conrad said. "It belonged to an SS general named Ludwig von Berg."

"The Baron of the Black Order?" Abdil's eyes grew wide.

Conrad nodded. "It's got a four-character alphabetic combination. Midas doesn't know the code. I do."

"One of the older boxes," Abdil said, leaning forward. "Is it in the seventeen or eighteen hundred series? It must be if Midas hasn't attempted to break it open."

"Yes."

"I thought so!" Abdil smiled. "Von Berg's box probably has a chemical seal that will break and destroy its contents if the combination is off by a single letter. Ha! How it must pain Midas to hold something in his hands and not be able to open it." Abdil leaned back in his chair and made a steeple with his fingers, contemplating the situation. "You think you can steal it out from under his nose if I can get you inside the bank."

"I do." Crafty minds like Abdil's always cut to the chase. That was why doing business with him was mostly straightforward—until it came time for Abdil's payback.

"Yes, yes, yes," Abdil said. "But no more words of this until the morning. The night is still young and the men too few for my girls."

"Thank you for your generosity, Abdil. But I'd really like to just climb into bed in my own room, if that's okay."

"But of course." Abdil snapped his fingers. "Layla!" A shapely young woman with an olive complexion appeared, carrying a digital clipboard. She displayed it to Abdil like a hostess showing the maître d' of a fine restaurant a map of tables.

"Suite 647 will suit our friend's tastes," Abdil said with a smile.

Ten minutes later, Conrad was shown his room. While considerably smaller than Abdil's penthouse, it didn't lack for amenities, including a young woman on his bed in nothing but a Miami Dolphins jersey.

"I'm Nichole," she said in an American accent. "What's your story?"

"Tired," he said, and decided it was best for everybody if she did the talking. "Tell me yours."

She was an American who had arrived in Gstaad a few months earlier after the Super Bowl with her boyfriend the professional football player. He'd left, she'd stayed. Blah, blah, blah.

Conrad concluded there was no way he could decline the present that Abdil had offered him. He didn't want to offend his host or make it appear that the nubile Nichole was anything less than a sexy vixen worthy of a royal harem.

"So which Dolphin am I competing against here?" he asked her.

"All of them." She giggled and pulled off her jersey.

19

Midas finally emerged from his bluestone kabbalah tank after six hours. He found Natalia in the bedroom, propped up on a pillow naked and playing with her BlackBerry. Natalia was his London mistress whenever Mercedes wasn't around, which at this point was for good.

"We have the private dining room at Roka reserved at nine o'clock," Natalia said. "I've got six friends coming. Two artists, three actors, and a fashion designer."

"We're not going anywhere tonight," Midas said flatly, and climbed into the bed.

She put the BlackBerry on the night table, revealing her full inviting breasts to him. "I'm still going to Paris, yes? I can't miss Mercedes's funeral. Every fashion icon in Europe will be there, and so will the press."

"I'm not taking you to Paris for the funeral of my official girlfriend," Midas said. "How would that look? Her father and family will be there. You can frolic with your friends another time."

Natalia seemed on the verge of pouting but thought better of it. "How long before we can go out together, just the two of us?" There was a slight demand in her voice.

"A week," he said, and she brightened considerably and kissed him voraciously. He felt himself respond in spite of his tiredness but still found himself distracted. "Tell me, have you news from any of your friends?"

Her friends were other Russian "it" girls prancing around the planet with billionaires and politicians of almost every nationality. Natalia, at twenty-six, had become a more formidable spymaster than his old superiors at the KGB.

She picked up her BlackBerry and said, "Little Nichole has a new friend in Gstaad."

An alarm rang in Midas's head, but he didn't know why. "Who's in Gstaad again?"

"Abdil Zawas. I think Nichole and the girls are stir-crazy. Like you, he doesn't get out often enough."

He ignored the displeasure in her voice. "That happens when you're on the international global terrorist watch list, like Abdil," he said. "Who is Nichole's new friend?"

"Some guy named Ludwig," she said, and showed him a picture that Nichole had sent her.

Midas sat up, grabbed the phone, and stared at the picture. He then used the phone to call Vadim, who sounded groggy when he picked up.

"I need you to get to Switzerland," Midas told him. "I've found Yeats."

20

The next morning Conrad woke up at the Sultan's Palace to find a handwritten note from Nichole on the pillow next to him. She had gone snowboarding on Videmanette Mountain and wanted to meet up at Glacier 3000 for lunch at two P.M. He looked at the clock and saw that it was already ten. He had slept over twelve hours.

There was a continental breakfast with a newspaper on the table. He put his feet into the slippers waiting at the bottom of his bed and tied on a robe. Then he poured himself some hot coffee from a silver pot and sat down at the table to look at the copy of the French daily *Le Monde*.

There was a picture of Mercedes on the front page with a headline: MONDAY SERVICES IN FRANCE FOR MERCEDES LE ROCHE, 32.

He found a smaller picture of himself on the jump on page eight. How on earth could Nichole not know he was a fugitive? He had to pray she hadn't seen it or never bothered to read a newspaper. He took comfort that the latter was more than probable.

Conrad figured Midas would have to show up at the funeral to put on a brave public face. Which gave him the perfect window: While Midas was in Paris at the funeral, Conrad would hit the bank in Bern.

Conrad put down the paper and saw that an envelope had been slipped under his door. He walked over and picked it up. Inside were architectural blueprints for the bank in Bern, marked up in French. An attached note from Abdil, written neatly in a female hand, instructed him to come up to the penthouse to meet with a Ms. Haury.

Conrad had no idea who Ms. Haury was, but he knew he had to keep moving forward and stay a step ahead of the Alignment, Interpol, and everybody else who was after him now. He had to get whatever was inside Baron von Berg's safe deposit box in Bern. It was his only bargaining chip.

He opened a closet filled with made-to-measure suits for him from Milan's Caraceni. The fabrics, fit for a prince, seemed to be cut from another world and fit perfectly.

A tailor would have had to work at gunpoint to pull this off so fast. Considering it was Abdil who had placed the order, Conrad could only wonder.

The two security guards posted outside his door escorted him down the hallway to the elevator. As they ascended to the penthouse, Conrad realized he couldn't have taken the elevator down to the lobby even if he'd wanted to.

The only way out of this palace was up.

* * *

Abdil's penthouse looked completely different in the full light of day. Conrad could have sworn it was fully refurnished, even the sculptures and art on the walls. Now it looked like a corporate boardroom of palatial proportions.

But there was no Abdil, only a curvy blonde standing next to the huge conference table, on which sat an ornate brass safe deposit box with a stainless steel door sporting four shiny brass dials and a brass keylock.

"I'm Dee Dee," the woman said, "the American CFO of Abdil's collectibles division. I understand from Mr. Zawas that you want to make a withdrawal from your box at the Gilbert et Clie bank in Bern."

"That's right," Conrad said, looking at the box with the four shiny brass dials. "I suppose it's too much to hope that this is the box in question."

"I'm afraid so," she said. "But the box you'll be opening will almost certainly be of this type. Take a seat."

Conrad sat down in a thronelike leather chair and listened to the polished Dee Dee explain the history of the box as if she were showcasing it on the Home Shopping Network.

"Any Swiss box with a number in the seventeen hundreds at Gilbert et Clie is among the most precious antique boxes in the vault," she told him. "That's because it's a triple-lock box. Very unusual. Only a few were manufactured in 1923 by Bauer AG in Zurich. Extremely rare."

Conrad touched the brass and steel box. It was only about three inches wide, two inches high, and seven inches long. Just how big was the secret Baron von Berg hoped to hide in such a small box?

"I see only two locks on the door," he said. "The four-dial combination lock and the keylock next to it."

"That's all you're supposed to see," she told him. "The distinctive combination lock you can't miss. It has four alphabetic brass dials for a total of 234,256 possible combinations. This is a lock you never forget."

Neither did Baron von Berg, thought Conrad, already imagining himself turning the four dials in sequence to line up the letters A-R-E-S. "What about the other two locks?"

Dee Dee nodded and said, "The two other lever locks share a mechanism housed inside the box's single keyhole."

"Two locks inside one keyhole?" Conrad repeated. "How does that work?"

"With two keys, of course," she said, and placed two keys on the table. One was silver, the other gold. "One bank key and one client key. Let me show you. I'll be the bank, you be the client."

She handed him the gold client key and picked up the silver bank key. "First things first. You need to open the combination lock. I've set the code for this box. It's OGRE."

Conrad turned the first dial to the letter "O," the second to the letter "G," the third to the letter "R," and the fourth to the letter "E," and heard an unmistakable click inside the box. "Wait a second," he said. "If the client has to open the combination lock first, before any keys are inserted, then the banker will know the combination to the client's box."

"Yes, but the client will change the combination before he closes the box," she told him. "It's like changing passwords on a computer system, only more secure." She held up the silver bank

key. "Now for the tumbler-lever lock. It has seven brass levers and two different bolt levers for a total of nine levers." She inserted the silver key into the single hole. "The bank key moves the three top levers and the top bolt lever to unblock the first part of the lock." She turned the key and then removed it. "This enables you, the client, to insert your key. Go ahead."

Conrad inserted his gold key into the hole and turned it until he felt it stop.

"Your key moves the four bottom levers and the bottom bolt lever," she said. "The bottom bolt lever is connected to the door bolt and the combination lock. That's the resistance you're feeling."

"Why won't it open?"

"Each dial of the alphabetical combination lock needs to be on the proper letter in order for you to be able to turn your key ninety degrees into a vertical position."

Conrad checked the dials again. They clearly spelled OGRE. "The dials are right. What's the problem?"

"The problem is that you're not finished yet," she told him. "Once the client key is vertical and the bolt is partially retracted, you need to scramble each dial again so your key can turn fully to the right and open the lock."

Conrad shook his head. *Von Berg, you paranoid son of a bitch,* he thought. Then again, he'd have watched his back, too, if he had worked for the world's craziest dictator.

Dee Dee seemed to feel she owed him an explanation. "Scrambling the combination before the door was opened was supposed to ensure that nobody else in the vault besides the banker could see the baron's secret combination while he was busy inspecting the contents of his safe deposit box."

"And if I make a mistake along the way somehow?"

"No second chances," Dee Dee said. "The box's chemical seal will break and destroy the contents. That's why a man as powerful as Roman Midas can own the bank and still not get to the contents of Baron von Berg's box. You have only one shot to open a box of this type. Go ahead. Give it a try."

Conrad turned the key, and the lock clicked open. He lifted the box lid and saw stacks of U.S. dollars—Ben Franklins. There had to be ten million dollars in the box. Conrad looked up to see Dee Dee lock eyes with him. "You will exchange the contents of your box for this one with Mr. Zawas after you leave the bank," she said, pausing to make sure they understood each other. Abdil Zawas didn't miss a trick; he wanted to give Conrad every incentive to come back after the job.

"I get it," Conrad said. "And if I don't show, I'm sure Mr. Zawas has a bigger box to stuff my corpse in."

"Mr. Zawas said that what you are after is not the contents of the box but the information those contents convey," Dee Dee said, and closed the box. "That being the case, he wants the contents for himself and is happy to pay you for them at this agreed-upon price."

"Fine, but there's only one problem," he told her. "I have the combination code, but I don't have a client key."

"The bank probably does," Dee Dee said. "Clients like Nazi generals who traveled to far-flung or dangerous parts of the world often allowed the banks to keep their keys because they didn't want to lose them. As long as they didn't forget their box number or combination code—or share them with anybody else—it was pretty foolproof."

"Even if I don't look like Baron von Berg's heir or, worse, I'm recognized on sight?"

"The bank's huissier will know you have business there as soon as you write down your box number, and she'll conclude from the seventeen hundred series that you're one of the bank's largest clients."

"No biometrics or anything?"

"Only in the movies," Dee Dee said. "The genius of the Swiss security system is that it's plain and transparent. You don't have to worry about somebody hacking your computer system and accessing your data or faking your biometrics. Locks, keys, and combinations beat the computer chip any day. Like the pyramids of Egypt that you raid, Swiss boxes will survive the ages. Think of this bank as just another tomb to raid, and you'll be fine."

"And when I present the box number and the huissier promptly informs Midas that someone has come to open the box?"

"Oh, they'll let you open the box," she said. "They just won't let you walk out of the bank with it. I can't help you there. But Mr. Zawas says you have the architectural blueprints to the bank."

"Yes," Conrad said. "But I don't know how accurate they are."

"I'm afraid that's a combination I can't help you with," she told him. "No doubt Sir Roman Midas has made some modifications to the bank not reflected in your schematics."

"No doubt," Conrad said.

21

It seemed to Serena that all of Paris had come to the church of Saint Roch to bid adieu to Mercedes Le Roche. Uniformed police held back the crowds lining Rue Saint-Honoré while office workers and residents in the buildings above leaned out their windows. All were straining to glimpse the celebrities arriving beneath a giant screen and loudspeakers broadcasting the funeral ceremony live.

Benito nudged the limousine ever closer to the hive of paparazzi ahead. Serena felt uneasy as she sank back in her seat and into the soft gray trouser suit and black trench coat that the people from Chanel had requested she wear to the funeral. A few years ago the Vatican's public relations agency had made some sort of bizarre agreement granting Chanel the right to dress Serena for affairs of state. It was an arrangement that she had always found ways to ignore. But having already packed her bags—and globes—for sunny Rhodes and not the cool rain of Paris, she'd had to reluctantly oblige this time.

The idea of a funeral as a fashion show, however, made her ill.

"Her funeral has a budget bigger than all her documentaries put together," she said. "Hardly anyone here knew her, and even fewer cared."

"It's Papa Le Roche's rank in French society that has brought out all the movie stars and other celebrities who have come to offer him their condolences," Benito said. "That would include you and President Nicolas Sarkozy."

"Where are the 'least of these' that Jesus talked about, Benito?"

"Watching the television, *signorina*."

Hopeless, she thought. Not only was she upset about what had happened to Mercedes, she was worried sick about Conrad and whether she'd ever see him again. She was also worried that she'd fail in Rhodes tomorrow. In fact, looking at the circus outside, she wondered if she and the Church had failed the world already with their complicity in this stagecraft of death. But Papa Le Roche had personally requested her presence for the family, and this was another chance to size up Roman Midas before Rhodes. Surely the grieving boyfriend would be on hand to eulogize the lover he had so ruthlessly slain.

She decided she desperately needed some fresh air. Cracking open her window just a bit, she could hear the crowds actually applauding every time a rocker or fashion designer stepped out of a limousine. As if this were some kind of award show. Which in a sense it was, she supposed, for Papa Le Roche.

"Skip the main entrance," she ordered Benito. "Take me around to the side."

They drove past the mob, turned a corner, and passed through a side gate, pulling up behind a black Volvo hearse. The hatch was up, and Serena could see Mercedes's casket in the back before the driver with an earpiece shut the door. He was going to go around the block to the crowds at the main entrance, where pallbearers would bring the casket into the church.

She was greeted at the side door by a young priest, who escorted her inside to the sanctuary. She was seated in the front row alongside a grief-stricken Papa Le Roche, a rather smug Roman Midas, and an expressionless President Sarkozy and his beautiful wife, Carla Bruni.

Serena offered her condolences to Papa Le Roche, who thanked her profusely for coming. Sarkozy and Midas looked at each other awkwardly, as if to say that today was certainly an unscheduled stop on the way to the EU peace summit on Rhodes tomorrow. Serena knew that neither had anticipated seeing the other before then. But while Sarkozy looked like he would have preferred not to be seen so close to the former Russian oligarch boyfriend of a woman who had died so violently, Midas seemed to relish his photo op next to the French president and among European society.

It was the French first lady, however, whose curious gaze after their kiss-kiss had made Serena the most uncomfortable. For some odd reason, it had prompted her to recall that she was ten years junior to Carla, who herself had been ten years junior to Sarkozy's second wife and thirteen years younger than his first. Then Serena saw the gray trouser suit beneath Carla's open black trench coat and realized that they were wearing the same outfit. Somebody at Chanel clearly hadn't cross-checked the cosmic social calendar.

Not that it bothered Serena. She was a linguist first and foremost, a nun second, and a celebrity who could raise funds for humanitarian aid a distant third. But she did feel bad for Karl Lagerfeld, the designer. He was sitting four pews behind with a row full of fashion icons, and when she glanced back to offer him a tender smile, he looked positively panic-stricken.

As the church bells tolled, six pallbearers in black Pierre Cardin suits carried Mercedes's casket into the church. They laid it feet toward the altar and then opened it to reveal a luminous Mercedes, frozen in time, with a rosary in her hands and flowers all around.

The tribute to Mercedes began with video clips of her childhood, followed by clips from her first documentary for French television. Several speakers read poems, and one played a vulgar song that was a favorite of hers. Then Midas rose to speak to his dearly departed.

Looking at Mercedes, he said, "You were a flower who faded too soon from this earth. But your sweet aroma will linger forever."

Serena wanted to gag. The duet of mourner and mourned did not go down well with her. She'd never liked eulogies staged during de facto state funerals, anyway. Especially when the deceased wasn't much of an angel or terribly sorry about it.

But what was she supposed to do? Stand up before all the bereaved, who right now were calculating their own odds of entering the pearly gates, and speak the truth, however awful, about Mercedes? Or was she supposed to bow to social convention and assure everyone in earshot that Mercedes was in heaven? Surely anybody who knew her, even her father, doubted it. She herself doubted that eulogies even belonged in church. After all, this was supposed to be a place where self-confessed sinners gathered in the holy presence of God. Not a stage for them to pat each other on the back for their illusory virtues.

What she especially didn't like was the feeling that none of them should have been there that day. Not the French president. Not her. Not Midas. And certainly not Mercedes. She wasn't supposed to die. None of this was supposed to have happened. But it did. Why?

Conrad. He'd happened. He had shown up at the Bilderberg party and put all the wheels in motion. He had turned her life upside down, like he always did, and it was never going to be put right until he and she were right.

It was her turn to speak.

She got up and placed a wheat sheaf on the coffin and repeated the eternal rest prayer. It was the most honest thing she could say. Not in French but in Latin, the way Mercedes likely would have wanted to tweak her proud nationalist papa, who liked to believe that Jesus was really a Gaul and not a Jew and that French was the language of angels.

*Réquiem ætérnam dona ei Dómine; et lux perpétua
lúceat ei. Requiéscat in pace. Amen.*

What Serena was saying was: "Eternal rest grant unto her, O Lord; and let perpetual light shine upon her. May she rest in peace. Amen." She could tell that the dignitaries in the front pew didn't understand, although they pretended they did. But several mourners in the fashion row nodded enthusiastically.

Father Letteron, wearing white and violet vestments, conducted the funeral Mass. There were flowers and candles all around. When it was over, Serena watched the shroud-draped coffin float out of the church before the hundreds of onlookers and cameras. Following behind was Father Letteron, who sang the antiphon "In Paradisum," a prayer that the holy angels would bear the immortal soul of Mercedes Le Roche to paradise.

If that meant television ratings, then perhaps Mercedes had indeed finally found her heaven.

The show inside over, Carla Bruni and Nicolas Sarkozy once again gave their condolences to Mercedes's father and then wordlessly marched outside to the waiting world. Midas took Papa Le Roche's arm and guided him out of the church. The rest of the mourners exited wherever they'd be sure to be photographed by the media.

Serena stood alone in the first pew, the hypocrisy of the world around her—and her place in it—feeling like a punch to her gut. She took a deep breath and stepped into the aisle only to be blocked by a young French aide. He looked red-faced with shame.

"I beg your forgiveness, Sister Serghetti," he said in French.

"Is there a problem?"

He hemmed and hawed. "I don't know how to say this."

Serena's patience had worn thin over the course of the funeral. "Spit it out."

"The first lady requests that you mourn a little longer in private," the Frenchman said, barely able to form the words. "She fears there might be, eh, speculation in the press that you have, eh, upstaged her in some way with your youth and beauty."

Holy Mother of God, she thought. But then she quickly confessed her angry, inner burst to God and forced an understanding smile to the aide. She could only imagine how many times each day this poor messenger got shot while bearing his little tidings of great vanity. And this was the church where Napoleon had mowed down royalist insurgents on the front steps.

"Quite all right," she said. "I'll just exit discreetly from the side."

He made the sign of the cross and bowed his head. "Thank you."

She did her best to make it to Benito and the car outside. She had to put Paris behind her and press on to Rhodes. But halfway out, her sadness and rage at the events of the morning began to overwhelm her, and she stopped to compose herself at the freestanding holy water stoup by the side door.

As she dipped the tips of her fingers into the marble basin and crossed herself, she could see her pale reflection in the water. Suddenly, the side door flew open, and she looked up to see a camera flash in her face.

22

Conrad paid the cabdriver and walked up the steps toward the venerable private banking firm of Gilbert et Clie. The bank was an austere granite building in Bern's Old Town, its presence marked only by a discreet brass plaque set in the wall.

A porter greeted Conrad as he entered the lobby with a leather weekender bag slung over his shoulder. The porter asked Conrad to state his business and then directed him to a reception area outside the private executive offices. Here, a smiling brunette in a red cashmere sweater took his Burberry raincoat. Her pale blue eyes seemed to linger in admiration of his athletic build beneath his three-piece suit. In the most exquisite French, she informed him that Monsieur Gilbert would see him in but a moment.

Conrad took a seat and surveyed the shabby but elegant reception area. The faces of several generations of Gilberts looked down from the oil paintings on the walls. For well over a century, the bank had remained in family hands, an outgrowth of their merchandising business. Why the family had sold the bank was just another one of the secrets it kept inside its vaults. It was one of only a few private banks in Bern, as most were in Geneva, and the only one with a French surname, not German. Like the other private banks, Gilbert et Clie was unincorporated and never published its balance sheets.

The mademoiselle returned and ushered Conrad into Gilbert's office. A tall, gray-haired man, elegant in boutonniere and black suit, rose from his desk. His resemblance to the faces in the paintings was unmistakable.

"A pleasure to meet you, Monsieur von Berg," Gilbert said in German, regarding Conrad keenly. "Please sit down and make yourself comfortable."

"Thank you," Conrad replied in English, dispensing with any Bavarian pretense.

An officer of the bank, a big, bald man whom Gilbert introduced as Monsieur Guillaume, stood silently by his side. He regarded Conrad warily from under his heavy eyelids.

"And how can I help you, Monsieur von Berg?" Gilbert asked.

"I've come to recover the contents of my grandfather's box."

Gilbert raised an eyebrow. "You have the key, of course?"

"No, you do," Conrad said. "Both of them. I have the box number and combination. And that's all that's required of me for this type of box."

Gilbert nodded. "You are correct. But you will forgive us for doing our best to protect the interests of our clients. You are the first person in seventy years to open"—he had to look at his computer screen—"box number 1740."

Gilbert called in his huissier—the brunette, who answered to the name of Elise—and handed her an envelope with the number on it. "Please escort Monsieur von Berg to the vault."

"*Oui*," she replied.

If they were letting her handle him, Conrad thought, that meant their guard was down—or they wanted him to let down his own.

Elise took him to the bank's antique elevator. As the polished brass cage began its slow two-hundred-foot descent to the vault beneath the bank, Conrad noted the Venetian mirrors on the elevator walls and the gray leather benches on three sides. He also noted a tiny hook in the corner of the floor. "This is an unusual elevator," he said. "It's the original?"

"Yes," she said. "It used to go down to an even lower level beneath the vault, where a secret tunnel to a park two blocks away would allow private clients like yourself to come and go without having to enter from the street. But the new owner filled the tunnel with concrete a few years ago."

Conrad nodded. Okay, so at least one alternative exit had been cut off.

The doors split open to reveal the safe deposit vault. The massive circular steel door was open, and a security guard standing beside a small desk nodded as Conrad followed Elise inside the vault.

As they walked past rows of gleaming boxes, Conrad could only imagine how much wealth was locked away here. Truly, this was the vault of the man called Midas. Finally, when they had reached the very back of the last row, Elise stopped and announced, "Box 1740."

Conrad turned to his right and saw the numbers. The box was at eye level. "That's right."

She took her key and inserted it into the box. "I will go first and then leave you to your box. You may take it to the private consultation room over there." She gestured to a small closet door, and Conrad nodded. "Then you will return the box, lock it, and call for me."

Conrad noted that she had failed to mention that if he got the combination wrong or blew the key toggle, the box's internal chemical lining would break and destroy whatever was inside.

Conrad eyed the brass doorplate with three brass fixtures. Left to right, there were the keylock, the four brass alphabetic dials set on top of a brass circular plate, and the small rectangular number plate that read 1740.

Conrad glanced at Elise, whose eyes grew ever wider as he turned the first dial to the letter "A," the second to the letter "R," the third to the letter "E," and the fourth to the letter "S." He heard an unmistakable click inside the box. He could also hear Elise catch her breath at the simplicity of the code.

"Now it is my turn," she said, and inserted the silver bank key into the keylock, gave it a twist, and then removed it. "I will leave you now."

Conrad waited until she was gone before he inserted his gold key into the lock. He turned it halfway and stopped. He then scrambled the dials and turned his key the full ninety degrees into a vertical position and felt the lock open with a satisfying click.

He opened the door and slid the box out. It felt light in his arms as he walked to the private consultation room. He grew anxious as he entered, shut the door behind him, and placed the box on the table.

He stared at it for a moment, took a deep breath, and with one hand opened the lid. As he stared inside the box belonging to SS General Ludwig von Berg, the Baron of the Black Order, he felt a pit form in his stomach. Then he reached in and removed the only item inside the box.

It was an old Swiss wristwatch.

23

A t that very moment, the prince of Egypt himself, Abdil
Zawas, was driving to the bank along Bern's River Aare in
his armored Mercedes Pullman Level B6 bulletproof limousine.

In addition to windows made of 42mm bulletproof, shatter-
proof, multiple-layer reinforced glass, the vehicle sported
special fuel tanks impervious to exploding upon impact from any
projectiles. The remote starting system allowed Abdil to remotely
detonate any explosive charges set to go off when the vehicle igni-
tion or door locks were activated. Just the sort of vehicle a man
of Abdil's stature—and Conrad Yeats's predicament—required
these days.

Abdil was en route to pick up Yeats from the bank, just in case
the American archaeologist had second thoughts about coming
back for his ten million dollars. Abdil's imagination was already
afire with speculation as to what SS General Ludwig von Berg
had secreted in Midas's bank—and the expression on Midas's
face when he finally saw the contents of the box in full display

aboard the new megayacht that Abdil was building to be the world's biggest.

What a moment that will be, Abdil thought with delight as the glass partition inside the limousine lowered and his driver, Bubu, said, "Police."

Abdil looked out his rear window to see a white Land Rover with orange stripes on the side and blue siren lights flashing. "See what he wants and don't make a scene," he said, and looked at his watch. He wanted to be parked outside the bank before Yeats came out.

Bubu pulled off the Aarstrasse at a riverfront park. The Land Rover parked directly in front of them. An officer stepped out in a dark raincoat and sunglasses. Abdil watched Bubu pull the registration papers from the glove compartment and lower his window.

"Yes?" asked Bubu as the officer approached the Mercedes.

The officer leaned through the open window. "The motorway pass on your windscreen is expired," he said, and shot Bubu in the head.

Instinct instantly took hold of Abdil, and he raised the glass partition in time to stop two bullets from the assassin, who removed his sunglasses to reveal an eyepatch and a face Abdil recognized as Midas's driver and bodyguard, Vadim. He knew the face from the fitness videos some of his girls used.

"You!" Abdil shouted into his two-way security intercom to the outside world for all to hear. "I am impregnable in here!" With a flourish, he picked up his phone and called his private emergency service.

A minute later, there was the comforting sound of a helicopter approaching, and Abdil started cursing Vadim, who had been patiently waiting outside. "Leave while you can, or the men jumping off that chopper will take your other eye for Bubu's sake."

Abdil heard a giant thud on the roof. The limousine lurched forward and back, then began to lift into the air. He looked out his window in time to see Vadim waving goodbye to him from the ground. Abdil started to shout as the chopper banked to the right with the entire limousine in tow, carrying him up and away.

24

Conrad frantically checked the box one more time, looking for any kind of hidden compartment or false bottom he may have missed. But there was none. There was only this damn watch.

He stared in dismay at Baron von Berg's sole piece of personal jewelry. The dial was stamped with ROLEX OYSTER and sported an unusual outer track of black-painted Roman numbers on top and Arabic numbers on the bottom. But that was all. In a vault filled with the wealth of dead Nazis, robber barons, deposed dictators, oil sheiks, and the like, why would SS General Ludwig von Berg have gone to such great lengths simply to preserve an old watch?

It felt like a bad joke.

Not only did Conrad have to get out of here in one piece, there was no way Abdil would believe that this watch was all he'd found, much less hand him millions in cash for it.

There had to be more to this watch than sentimental value to a crazy Nazi.

Just like the name of the Roman god of war carried some meaning for Baron von Berg, so, too, did the number 1740 for the box. The same had to be true of this watch, which had its hour and minute hands stopped at midnight—or noon. That was no accident. The watch didn't stop winding down at that exact minute. Von Berg had left it that way.

A crazy thought seized Conrad. Von Berg may have been insane, but he was a military man, too. Military men, as Conrad knew all too well from growing up with the Griffter, used military time. And 1740 hours meant 5:40 P.M.

Conrad carefully pulled out the watch's side-turning knob and slowly adjusted the hands until the hour hand reached the number five on the dial and the minute hand reached the number eight.

When he pushed the thumb knob down again, the watch's two-piece screw-back case fell open. A coin hit the table and rolled onto the floor.

Conrad quickly snatched it up. It was an ancient Roman coin with a Caesar's bust and an eagle on the back. It was oddly familiar; it reminded him of the Tribute Penny that Serena wore around her neck. But that medallion was one of a kind.

Or was it?

Conrad quickly inserted the coin snugly beneath the gears of the watch and replaced the back case, inside of which was stamped OYSTER WATCH CO. Then he strapped the watch to his wrist, closed the box, and stepped out into the vault with his shoulder bag. Without bothering to call for Elise, he slid the box back into its slot and walked out.

The security guard by the desk was already calling upstairs by the time Conrad stepped into the old brass elevator and let the doors close. As soon as they did, he dropped to the floor and reached into his bag to remove a knife.

He cut along the hidden seams beneath the carpet and then pulled the tiny hook in the corner he had seen to reveal a lower compartment. That was where the VIPs had entered and exited in secret from the old tunnel Midas had sealed up.

Conrad had seen this type of elevator only once before—Hitler's old Eagle's Nest retreat atop Mount Kelstein in Bavaria. The Nazis had bored a four-hundred-foot elevator shaft in the center of the mountain. That 1938 brass elevator was also a double-decker. Hitler and his important guests rode the brass-lined upper cabin to the top while his guards and supplies for the house rode unseen in the bottom cabin.

Conrad placed an explosive puck on the floor of the upper cabin and dropped into the bottom cabin and pulled the trapdoor shut. He then pulled out his hazmat gas mask and waited in the dark with a small detonator in his hand.

When the elevator stopped and the door in the top cabin opened in the bank's lobby, he heard shouts from security guards at the sight of the empty compartment. He then pressed the button and exploded the puck containing the knockout gas sufentanil. There was more shouting, and a body dropped with a crash in the cabin above him.

It took him a minute longer than he expected to pop the trapdoor open, but then he crawled out into the lobby and stood up, hearing loud hacking coughs as he stepped over the bodies.

The porter at the front door had managed to press a silent alarm before going down, and when Conrad finally stepped outside and ripped off his mask, the sound of sirens blared.

He walked quickly down the street, turned a corner, and hailed a cab. He was opening the door when the sound of a helicopter forced him to look up. To his astonishment, he saw the screaming face of Abdil Zawas pressed against the window of his limousine before it disappeared with the chopper over the roof of the UBS building.

Conrad quickly climbed into the back of the cab and said, "American embassy."

25

Midas stood in what he considered to be his rightful place next to the French president, his wife, and Papa Le Roche at the curb outside Saint Roch as they silently watched pallbearers load Mercedes's flag-draped coffin into the back of the hearse, which would take it to the more intimate burial service at the family's tomb at Père Lachaise Cemetery.

Midas did his best to look somber before the crowds and cameras, but those next to him had more practice, and he had to work at keeping his chest from swelling with pride from his arrival at the pinnacle of European society. He'd had to buy his way in with the Brits, and even then his acceptance had felt forced. The Parisians were far more accommodating of his violent reputation, which for them only seemed to add a dash of romance to his otherwise mysterious background.

"Mercedes did love her rogues," he heard Papa Le Roche repeat outside, although the plural reference reminded Midas of Conrad Yeats, and the thought that he and Yeats had shared Mercedes disturbed him. He took comfort in the knowledge that shortly, Yeats would be joining the dearly departed in the afterlife. It was all Midas could do to keep from checking his BlackBerry for word from Vadim in Bern.

Papa Le Roche then clasped arms with Sarkozy, Carla, and Midas. To great effect, he upstaged Midas by climbing into the front of the hearse himself—there was room for only one passenger, presumably the most important man in Mercedes's life—to ride with his daughter to the cemetery.

As soon as the black Volvo hearse drove off down the Rue Saint-Honoré past the throngs of onlookers held back by police and metal fences, Midas turned to Sarkozy. "Are you going to the burial?"

The French president shook his head. "Rhodes calls. The world is a mess. Turmoil in the markets. War in the Middle East. We do what we can. I am to give the opening and closing presentations at the summit. I am but a bookend."

"I will see you there, then," said Midas, and clasped arms with Sarkozy and then enjoyed a double kiss with Carla before France's first couple climbed into their presidential limousine.

As Midas watched their motorcade drive off, led by police on motorcycles, he felt the pleasant vibration of power in the form of his BlackBerry calling. He picked up the call from Vadim. "So we are rid of Yeats once and for all?"

There was a pause on the other end. Midas didn't like it. "We got Zawas. But Yeats escaped."

Midas felt stomach acid flare up in the back of his throat. "And the contents of the box?"

"Yeats."

Midas dropped the phone and leaned on a loitering pallbearer for support. Several cameras captured the moment, confusing the expression of loss on his face to be one for Mercedes. The Rhodes summit started tomorrow, and Midas needed that coin to join the Thirty. Even the *Flammenschwert* couldn't help that. All his leverage would be gone by Friday.

Midas scanned the crowds and saw Serena making for the side entrance and her car. He took a breath, stood up, and thanked the concerned onlookers. "I'll be fine. Life goes on. Thank you."

He retreated back to the church and then broke into a run to catch Serena before she drove off.

26

The U.S. embassy in Bern was at Sulgeneckstrasse 19, and Conrad's cabdriver took his sweet time getting across the city's River Aare. Conrad clocked it on his new official Black Order Rolex: almost nine minutes to make it over a four-lane bridge, merge into the far-right lane, and reach the next intersection just in time for the light to turn red.

"What are you waiting for?" Conrad demanded. "Take a right."

"This isn't America," the Syrian driver replied rudely in English. "There is no turn on red light unless permitted by green arrow."

"I'll pay you extra."

The Syrian looked over his shoulder at him with contempt. "I am a law-abiding citizen."

Two minutes later, they turned right onto Monbijoustrasse and then took another immediate right onto Giessereiweg. Two minutes after that, the road turned into Sulgenrain, and they followed it until finally turning left onto Sulgeneckstrasse.

The street was one-way for security purposes; Conrad spotted the embassy about two hundreds yards down the street on the right. It was a white office building surrounded by an ugly security fence.

"I'll look for your picture inside," Conrad said as he paid the driver and watched him drive off.

He started walking quickly to the gate. He was half a block away and passing a paid parking area when a Swiss police Land Rover started to drive slowly alongside him. As soon as the window lowered, Conrad didn't wait for the arm to pop out with a pistol. He dove behind a parked car just in time to see Vadim's ugly face in the car's side mirror before Vadim blew the mirror off.

Conrad made a dash the opposite way up the one-way street, using the parked cars as a hedge. The Land Rover tried to back up, but oncoming traffic put a stop to that, and Vadim had to jump out and pursue on foot.

Conrad cut across the corner of Sulgeneckstrasse and Kapellenstrasse and ran downhill about three hundred yards to a blue arrow tram leaving the stop at Monbijou. He bought a ticket from the vending machine and hopped on just as Vadim ran up from behind, no doubt noting that it was Tram 9 Wabern heading for the city's train station just two stops away.

The tram began to snake beneath the storybook archways and through the arcades of old Bern. Conrad caught his breath as he stood among the tourists and commuters. The next tram was ten minutes away, so he had to assume Vadim would drive like a madman to beat him or radio someone at the end of the line.

As much as he hated the idea, he had to call Packard and ask for a secure pickup. He reached inside his pocket for the Vertu cell phone that Abdil had given him and realized that he must have lost it when he dove for cover near the embassy.

All too soon the tram stopped at Bubenbergplatz, opposite the main train terminal. Conrad had to make a run for it and hop a train out of Switzerland. Between the Swiss police, Interpol, and the Alignment, he was dead if he stayed here.

He scanned the plaza and was making a beeline for the station when he saw the Land Rover pull up and Vadim get out. He also saw legitimate police cars at the entrance and a number of patrolmen on foot talking into their radios.

In a heartbeat, he doubled back in the opposite direction to the towering Heiliggeist church. Built in the early 1700s, the Heiliggeistkirche, or Holy Spirit Church, was supposed to be the finest example of Protestant church architecture in Switzerland, with its magnificent baroque interior and encircling gallery.

The choir was rehearsing the "Easter Oratorio," as composed by Johann Sebastian Bach in 1735. Several soloists in costume sang the parts of the two Marys and the disciples who followed them to the empty tomb of Jesus. They were accompanied by three trumpets, two oboes, timpani, strings, and the church's massive organ. The musicians were considerably younger than the choir, the church organist considerably older.

Conrad took a seat next to a young man wearing angel wings and watched the rehearsal. The angel handed him a flyer. It was in German and titled OSTER-ORATORIUM. Conrad had to think up something. *"Sprechen Sie Deutsch?"* he asked the angel.

"No, dude, I'm American," the angel said. "Semester abroad. Chicks dig this shit. So do guys. But I dig chicks. So don't dis my wings."

Perfect, Conrad thought, glancing around the vast church. He looked up at the oblong pastel ceiling high above the rows of curved wooden pews. It was held up by fourteen sandstone columns. "Do you actually have a part?"

"I get to announce the resurrection and that Jesus is alive."

"That's awesome."

"Yeah, and then I get to score with the second Mary Magdalene over there from Copenhagen."

"Never going to happen," Conrad said with an earnestness born of experience that shocked even him. "Hey, my phone battery is gone. Can I borrow yours?"

The angel handed him a Nokia and said, "Got an emergency?"

"You could say that," Conrad said. "I definitely need to call God."

"Well, you've come to a house of prayer, so pray."

"That's okay. I've got her number."

27

Benito had the engine running by the time Serena reached the limousine. Her phone rang. It was Conrad.

"Where on God's green earth are you?" she demanded as she climbed in the back.

Conrad said, "It's time we lay our cards on the table. Meet me at the Villa Feltrinelli at Lake Garda tonight at six. You're the Baroness von Berg."

"You must be joking," she said. "I'm supposed to be in Rhodes tomorrow."

"Then you better know what's on the agenda," he said, and hung up.

She met Benito's eyes in the rearview mirror and said, "What's our status on the globes?"

"Brother Lorenzo says they are prepared and will arrive separately in Rhodes as art for the exhibit at the Palace of the Grandmaster. By keeping them roped off, he feels closer inspection will wait until after the summit."

Serena's mind was racing while the engine ran in neutral and Benito waited for her signal. Lake Garda was in northern Italy, a good three hours by plane, train, or automobile. And she had duties to perform at Mercedes's grave site.

"Get me a seaplane, Benito. I'm going to fly myself to Rhodes— after an unscheduled stop. You get yourself back to the Vatican and accompany the globes to Rhodes. Don't let them out of your sight."

Benito nodded and moved the car into drive just as Serena's door opened and Midas climbed in next to her.

"What are you doing, Midas?" she nearly screamed.

Benito hit the brakes, and before she and Midas even stopped bouncing, he had a 9mm Beretta pointed over the front seat at Midas.

Midas put up his hands and said, "I needed a ride to Père Lachaise for the burial. I thought I could take the opportunity to seek your spiritual counsel. Look, I have none of my aides with me."

"You mean assailants."

"Whatever."

Serena sighed, exchanged a glance with Benito in the mirror, and nodded.

They drove slowly out the side, past a gate, and onto Rue Saint-Honoré, where the crowds had quickly dispersed and the boutiques had opened for business again, as if the orgy of stagecrafted grief had never happened.

"Conrad Yeats stole something of great value from me," Midas said firmly.

"Mercedes will be missed," Serena said calmly.

"I am speaking of the contents of a safe deposit box in Bern," Midas said. "Yeats broke into my bank and stole my box."

Serena realized that she had to meet with Conrad. "Well, you'll need to employ better security to reassure your other customers."

"No, you'll need to get it back for me and kill Yeats when he contacts you."

"Why would he do that?"

"Don't play me for a fool. Mercedes told me everything about your sordid relationship with the man. So did Sorath."

With the mention of Sorath, Midas wanted her to know that he was a member of the Alignment and that he knew she was, too.

"All the more reason for Sorath to be upset to learn of your loss. If you tell me what it is, maybe I can help you."

Midas turned his gaze from the Dei medallion dangling around her neck to the Eiffel Tower in the distance. "A few minutes ago I wondered if Sorath was Sarkozy, that pompous French prick."

"If you're asking me whether he's the Antichrist, no," Serena said. "But I'm sure a man like Sarkozy would give the position some serious consideration if it were offered to him. You, too."

"And the pope?"

"The Vatican can't be bought off like the Russian Orthodox Church."

"No, it was bought off far earlier by Constantine and the Dei," Midas snarled. "And just who do you think you are? You're a little ecclesiastical whore of the pope, a false prophet if there ever was one."

Serena let that one go and allowed silence to fill the car. They were on the Boulevard de Ménilmontant. Soon they'd reach the cemetery. "I'm sorry, you were asking me for help?"

Midas looked at her with quiet rage. "I hope for your sake you have the globes."

She retorted, "I hope for your sake you have whatever it is you think that Conrad Yeats stole from you."

"Oh, I will," Midas said. "Because you will take it from him after you kill him. Only then will your loyalty to the Alignment no longer be in question."

"And yours isn't?"

"I have leverage, Sister Serghetti," Midas said. "It is the most important tool in business. It is having something the other party wants. I have something Sorath and the Alignment not only want but desperately need."

"And what would that be?"

He smiled. "You think you have something the Alignment needs in those globes from Solomon's Temple. But here, too, I have leverage: I know you don't have both of them. The Americans still possess one. And if two globes show up in Rhodes, I will know that one of them is a fake. And then where will you be?"

Serena felt a chill. Midas had sources within the Pentagon or the Dei, maybe both. If the Pentagon, her thoughts turned to Packard; if the Dei, they immediately went to Lorenzo. Either way, her plan to unmask and ultimately thwart the Alignment was at risk—along with any future she hoped to share with Conrad in this lifetime.

"Benito, I think Sir Midas is threatening to kill me."

"*Sí, signorina.* The family will take care of him."

"The cardinals will be thanking God in their prayers once you're gone, Sister Serghetti," said Midas. "Or do they still call you Sister Pain in the Ass behind your back in Vatican City?"

"I think Benito was referring to *his* family," Serena said, then lowered her voice to a whisper for effect. "The Borgias."

The name clearly registered with Midas. The Borgias had been the Church's first crime family in the Middle Ages and included eleven cardinals, three popes, and a queen of England. They killed for power, money, and wanton pleasure. That was centuries ago, of course, and Benito's branch of the family had long left the Church to establish the Mafia.

"You crazy bitch," Midas said. "You play us all off each other. The Americans, the Russians, the Alignment, the Mob. You are the devil."

"Well, we all have our issues," she said, looking him in the eye. "I'm curious, Midas. What exactly is the Alignment promising you? You already have more money than just about anybody else in the world. And you seem to recognize what the Church has known for centuries—that those in power are more often defined by history rather than the other way around."

"A new world order is coming," Midas said. "The old order, including the Church, will pass away."

They drove past the Métro station Philippe Auguste and through the main entrance of the Père Lachaise Cemetery, which had been established by Napoleon in 1804.

Serena took advantage of the scenery. "I've heard that before." She made a point of looking at his trembling hand and then out

her window at the rows of crosses, tombstones, and burial monuments. "What good is the new world order, Midas, if you're not
around to enjoy it?"

Midas smiled. "That is this thing, is it not?"

"Yes," she said as Benito parked behind the convoy of cars
trailing the black Volvo hearse. "I know where I'm going when I
die. So, unless there's another heaven I don't know about, where are
you going to end up?"

Midas's eyes were black and shining with a secret he seemed
to be dying to tell her. He leaned over. "I have news for you," he
whispered. "There won't be a heaven or an afterlife."

She looked at him curiously. He seemed more certain of what
he was telling her than he had seemed of anything else.

"Who knows," Midas added. "Even you might enjoy the new
world order and forget all about Conrad Yeats. While you've been
worrying about him, he certainly hasn't been worrying about you."

Midas pulled out his BlackBerry and played a video clip from
a private file on his smartphone's memory card. The video showed
Conrad frolicking in bed with a young girl in a Miami Dolphins
jersey. The time stamp at the bottom of the frame showed that it
was barely forty-eight hours old.

"That's enough, Midas."

"Good." Midas put away the phone in triumph. "Then we
are agreed. You kill Conrad Yeats to prove your loyalty to the
Alignment and bring what Yeats stole from me to Rhodes."

"Or else?" she asked.

"Or else I'll expose your sham with the globes, and it will be
your funeral I'll eulogize at next week."

28

GRAND HOTEL A VILLA FELTRINELLI
LAKE GARDA, ITALY

It was half past four when Conrad's Town Car turned off the country road and onto a long private drive lined with stately palms and cypresses. The end of the gravel drive opened like a dream to reveal the majestic Villa Feltrinelli and its octagonal tower overlooking the waters of Lake Garda.

The Feltrinelli family, who made their fortune in lumber, had built the villa at the end of the nineteenth century. By the middle of the twentieth century, in the waning days of World War II, the villa became famous as the final residence of Italian dictator Benito Mussolini before his execution. In the twenty-first century, Swiss management had turned the Villa Feltrinelli into one of Europe's most private, secure, and romantic luxury hotels, an unspoiled paradise far from the cares of the outside world.

The perfect place, Conrad thought, *for a rendezvous with Serena.*

A young Swiss miss welcomed him as Baron von Berg in the grand entry hall with a bouquet of rosebuds. Conrad looked past the circular sofa and carved wooden benches to the marble staircase with tall stained-glass windows and gilded mirrors. There were twenty-one guest rooms in the main villa, including the Magnolia Suite where Mussolini had slept. For Serena's sake, Conrad had booked the private boathouse outside the main villa, away from the other guests.

A sporty Italian bellman named Gianni took Conrad's weekender bag that he had purchased in nearby Desenzano after his six-hour ride from Bern involving two trains, one passport check, and one transfer in Milan.

"*Guten Tag*, Baron von Berg," said Gianni in passable German. "Where is the baroness?"

"She has her own ride."

They walked outside the covered pergola and past the pool with ducks and terraced gardens toward the lakeside boathouse. Two couples were enjoying afternoon tea on the lawn while a third played a game of croquet. Nothing was forced, including the prosecco offered to Conrad on a floating tray. Life and love seemed to flow quite naturally here.

"We have our own yacht for cocktail cruises," Gianni told him. "You can arrange for a motor launch to take you and the baroness around the lake and even explore the medieval castle at Sirmione."

"That sounds wonderful, Gianni," Conrad said, sipping his drink.

The boathouse was spacious enough, with dark wood paneling and eggshell linens and upholstery. Its tall windows with sheer lace curtains offered a spectacular view of the lake.

Once the young bellman had closed the door on his way out, Conrad turned to find a dessert tray of lemon mousse sprinkled with fruit and edible flowers, a jasmine-scented candle burning on the nightstand, and rose petals strewn throughout the marble bathroom.

The only thing missing from this perfect romantic scene was Serena.

He looked at the antique Rolex, his gift from Baron von Berg. It was almost five o'clock, and Serena's seaplane was due to land on the lake any minute now.

Conrad removed the watch and adjusted the dial until the Roman coin fell onto the table. He then pulled out a set of two books titled *Coinage and History of the Roman Empire* that he had picked up at a rare coin shop in Desenzano. The pages were thin, the lines single-spaced, and the font small, which made reading hard, but he found what he needed.

Conrad picked up the ancient Roman coin.

It looked almost like an American quarter, with Caesar instead of George Washington on one side and an eagle on the other. But this eagle looked quite distinctive, with a club on its right and a palm frond on its left. Indeed, it looked just like the medallion Serena wore around her neck.

He took a closer look at the letters engraved around the coin's rim:

UROUIERAS KAIASULOU

Instantly, he knew the translation. He had come across it on coins during his digs beneath the Temple Mount in Jerusalem:

OF TYRE, THE HOLY AND INVIOLATE

He flipped to a page with the heading "Judas's Thirty Pieces of Silver" and a quote from the Gospel of Matthew:

> Then one of the 12, called Judas Iscariot, went
> unto the chief priests, and said unto them, "What
> will ye give me, and I will deliver him unto you?"
> And they covenanted with him for 30 pieces
> of silver.

The book said the coin was a so-called Shekel of Tyre, or temple tax coin. It was the only currency accepted at the Jerusalem temple, so it was most likely the coinage with which Judas had been paid for betraying Jesus Christ.

The bust on the front didn't belong to any Roman emperor, Conrad realized, putting away the coin books. It belonged to Melqarth, the god of the Phoenicians, with a laurel wreath around his head like Caesar's. Better known as Baal in the Old Testament. Sacrilege to Orthodox Jews, to be sure. But these coins were the only ones close enough to pure silver to be accepted at the temple. Roman coins were too debased.

He searched for a date on the coin. He found it on the reverse side, left of the eagle and just above its club.

EL

That was the year 35 C.E. on the Julian calendar—or 98 B.C., according to contemporary calendars. Well within the time of circulation during Jesus' lifetime.

It was certainly not the Tribute Penny that Jesus had used to advise followers to go ahead and give their tax money to the state but their whole hearts to God. If anything, the shekel represented quite the opposite—man-made religion that trusted not in the God of heaven but in Caesar and the power structure of this world. The penny was blessed, in short, and the shekel cursed.

Like the Dei.

Conrad's concentration was broken by the sound of a prop engine. He looked out to the lake and saw Serena flying in. Hopefully with some answers, for once.

29

Serena swung her seaplane over the treetops and came in for her final approach on the shimmering waters of Lake Garda. The breathtaking Villa Feltrinelli rose on the distant shore like a fairy castle. The sheer audacity of Conrad's selection of such a romantic locale, and this while he was on the run, amazed and angered her. A virgin like her wouldn't last the night at a place like this, especially with a man like him.

She'd flown her first high-wing Otter as a missionary in the Australian outback. Later, she'd flown in the African bush. This plane was a propeller-driven DHC-3, powered by a single six-hundred-horsepower Pratt & Whitney Wasp radial and fitted with floats, just like the type she'd used in the Andes during her work with the Aymara tribe. That was where she'd first met Conrad, on Lake Titicaca, the highest lake in the world and her personal favorite. No doubt it was an association he had hoped to evoke here.

She prayed in advance for God's wisdom and strength to do what her mission required of her. The only problem was that she had so *many* missions these days, often at cross purposes. Her challenge here, she had to remind herself, was to steal from Conrad whatever he'd stolen from Midas, find out what else he knew, and then somehow get rid of him in such a way as to satisfy the Alignment and her own conscience.

Keeping her vows of purity, therefore, was the least of her worries.

She eased back on the throttle and put the Otter down into the water. The water was calm and gold in the late-afternoon sun, perfect to land on because of the enclosed nature of the lake. To her starboard, the hills looked like black paper cut out against twilight. *Lots of peace and quiet here,* she thought, which suited her just fine after the events of recent days and the days to come.

She taxied toward the boathouse in front of the villa. A man stood on the stone jetty with a rope tie. It wasn't Conrad. It was a porter from the villa who came alongside the Otter to tie it down.

She switched off the engine and climbed down to the plane's float. It was definitely more balmy and sensual here than in Paris at this time of year. She steadied herself for a second under the wing while she reached back into the cabin to pull out her little leather backpack. Then she took the extended hand of the young porter, who helped her step onto the jetty.

"Baroness von Berg. The baron is waiting for you."

I'm sure he is, she thought, and nodded with a smile but said nothing as she followed him down the jetty toward the villa. She could see that the Villa Feltrinelli offered everything a couple like her and the baron could want.

She looked out at the lake. If the porter knew who she was, he was saying nothing. That was one thing she had to give Conrad: Even if every member of the staff thought the holy Mother Earth had come for a secret tryst with her lover, and hazarded a guess this was her habit, nobody else would know. As much as she wanted to avoid the appearance of moral failure, this scenario was what it was, and people could think what they wanted.

He led her to the boathouse, which apparently was an even more private suite than those that occupied the main villa. *Bravo, Conrad*, she thought, and thanked the porter.

"Gianni," he offered helpfully.

She nodded. "Like the legendary soccer player Gianni Rivera?"

"*Sì!*" he said, eyes wide. "I was named after him."

Serena smiled. These days Rivera was a member of the European Parliament for the Uniti nell'Ulivo party. She followed Canadian hockey more closely than European football, but she knew enough about Rivera to know that he'd been the Wayne Gretzky of soccer in his day, able to instinctively know where the ball was going before it went there. It was an ability she had tried to cultivate in her own arena, where religion and politics squared off.

She switched to fluent Italian for Gianni's benefit: "We'll need his kind of passing game this year if our team is going to have a shot at the World Cup."

Gianni nodded enthusiastically as the door to the boathouse opened.

A remarkably gorgeous Conrad stepped out and handed Gianni a wad of Euros. "*Tausend dank,*" he said, and waved Gianni away.

Gianni reluctantly walked off to the main villa, glancing back every now and then as if afraid to leave the baroness in the clutches of the barbarian Baron von Berg.

"I think he's in love," Conrad told her, and looked at her with sparkling eyes. "We all are."

Without warning, he kissed her full on the lips. She threw both arms around his neck and kissed him back passionately. She felt him lift her up like a groom his bride and carry her across the threshold into their suite, where he nudged the door shut behind them and set her down.

She was breathless as they stared at each other, each waiting for the other to break the mood with some glib remark to coolly reestablish the uncrossable cosmic chasm that fate had always thrown up between them.

It's always me, she thought. *I'm always the one to push him away.*

But she didn't want to push him away. She wanted him to do it, prayed to God that he would do it. And Conrad, who could read her soul like one of his glyphless mysteries of antiquity, obliged for her sake and not his.

"Show me yours and I'll show you mine," he said.

She blinked. "What?"

He reached up to her neck, his fingers caressing her skin ever so gently. She put her own hand to his. But then he yanked the Dei medallion off her neck, leaving a slight red burn line.

"Conrad!" she yelled, and gripped her throat while he dangled the medallion in front of her face, his eyes on fire.

"So what's Her Holiness of the Roman Catholic Church doing holding the face of Baal between her breasts?" he demanded.

"I know." She swallowed hard. "It's not the Tribute Penny of Jesus."

"No, it's a Shekel of Tyre. Just like one of those thirty goddamn pieces of silver Judas took to betray *your* Lord and Savior."

"No, Conrad," she gasped, trying to catch her breath. "It *is* one of the Judas coins."

30

Conrad looked at Serena across the table outside the boat-house. She was clearly enjoying the lakeside dinner person-ally prepared for them by Chef Stefano Baiocco: fish soup with tiny squids, Parma ham with prawns and artichoke hearts, Lake Garda white fish called corégone, and homemade tagliolini with pesto. All paired with the most amazing wines.

When all the plates were cleared and the sun had finally set, Conrad sat back and listened to her telling him everything.

According to the New Testament gospels, Judas had sold out Jesus to the ruling religious council of the Jews, the Sanhedrin, for thirty pieces of silver. Those shekels came out of their temple tax coffers. After the Sanhedrin turned Jesus over to the Romans and it was clear that the Romans were going to kill Jesus by cru-cifixion, Judas was filled with remorse and hanged himself. Before he did, however, he returned to the temple and threw his money at the priests. The priests, recognizing at this point that the shek-els were blood money, couldn't deposit them back into the holy temple treasury. So they used the money for charity. They bought some land and turned it into a cemetery for paupers who couldn't afford a proper burial.

"That much I know," Conrad said. "Go on."

According to the tradition of Dominus Dei, Serena told him, the man who sold his land to the Sanhedrin used the thirty pieces of silver to purchase another piece of land. This land he purchased from St. Matthew, the former tax collector and disciple of Jesus who wrote the authoritative gospel account of Judas's coins. The land Matthew sold, moreover, was land that Judas had purchased for himself with money he had stolen from the disciples' slush fund.

Conrad knew that apocryphal traditions were hard to authenticate and too often served the agendas of those who propagated them, so he was suspicious. "Why would Matthew even want that money?" he asked her. "What did he do with it?"

"Church tradition doesn't really speculate on what happened to Matthew, but somehow the coins got to Rome," she told him. "The Dei were established in the courts of Caesar well before St. Paul arrived in Rome and was beheaded by the emperor Nero. They were the secret Christians among Caesar's staff and praetorian guard that Paul referred to in his last letters from prison before his execution."

"So they just watched Paul's head roll down the palace steps?" Conrad asked dubiously. "Nice friends there, Serena. But I guess you have to save your own ass before you save the world. Is that what Jesus said? No, I guess not."

"I'm not excusing the Dei, Conrad. I'm just telling you their history. Because the Roman emperors established themselves as gods, any Christian who claimed to serve another god faced death. So instead of using the old codes of crosses and fishes, which Rome's imperial intelligence services had cracked, they used the silver shekels to identify themselves to each other."

"And how long did that work?" Conrad asked.

Serena gave him a funny look. "For about three hundred years, at which point the emperor Constantine converted to Christianity and it became the official religion of the Roman Empire."

"And completely corrupted by power," Conrad added. "At some point these coins stopped being heirlooms passed along after death. They became objects to be possessed by killing their owners in order to move up in the ranks of the Alignment."

"I don't know when it started, exactly," she said. "Maybe with the Knights Templar."

"What the hell are *you* doing with these people, Serena? That's what I want to know. Especially after you pledged your undying love to me under the Mall in Washington, D.C., only to ditch me and steal that terrestrial globe."

She seemed to visibly tense up at the mention of the globe, and Conrad was glad to see it was still a sore point with her, too.

"The Alignment had targeted the U.S. ever since its founding and was on the verge of taking over the American republic from within until you stopped it," she began. "But when you left me alone there under L'Enfant Plaza with the globe, the secret seal of the United States, and those creepy Houdon busts of America's 'other' founding fathers, I didn't know if you were going to succeed in stopping the Alignment and come back for me."

"So you stole the globe."

"If the Alignment had succeeded in taking over the federal government, they would have had both globes, Conrad. I couldn't take the risk, especially after I recognized the face of one of those busts. The family resemblance, together with my knowledge of his history, led me to realize that Cardinal Tucci of Dominus Dei was a member of the Alignment. I had no idea that the Dei itself was an organ of the Alignment until after Tucci's suicide and his passing of the mantle, or rather medallion, to me."

It took an incredible amount of willpower, but Conrad maintained an even tone of voice. "You didn't have to stay."

"I was just supposed to run off with you, make love, have babies, and let the world go to hell?"

"Yeah, if the alternative is hooking up with the devil."

"Sometimes you have to join them to lick them, Conrad. The Dei is just one thread of the Alignment, the ecclesiastical thread, represented by one coin—mine. Destroying my cell would do little to hurt the larger organization. You know the Alignment traces itself much further back than the Church, to before the Egyptians and even Atlantis. They use empires and religions and new world orders like locusts consuming one host after the other. Now these coins are in the hands of the world's most powerful political, financial, and cultural leaders."

Conrad sighed. There was no way she was going to bed with him tonight. "So you want to put names to faces."

"No, I want to put faces to the names I've got."

She explained that the Alignment had organized itself along the ranks of angels. There was the grandmaster at the top, surrounded by a council of thirty "knights." In addition to possessing one of the original Judas coins, each knight had a divine name that described his or her nature and role within the organization.

"Sorath is the name of the grandmaster," she told him. "Sorath is a fallen angel whose number, Rome believes, is 666. I have no idea who he is, but I assume he will be in Rhodes, where the Council of Thirty will be gathered for the first time in three hundred years."

"Why now?" Conrad asked, although he knew that the recovery of the legendary technology of Atlantis in the *Flammenschwert* was certainly one factor. But he suspected it wasn't the deciding factor.

Serena shrugged. "I guess I'll find out when I get there."

There was something she wasn't telling him, but he couldn't put his finger on it. "What about you, Serena? What's your name?"

"Naamah," she said, looking down. "The fallen angel of prostitution who is more pleasing to men than to God."

Conrad decided he didn't want to go there in this discussion. She was already scaring the hell out of him. "And Midas?"

"Well, he's clearly inherited Baron von Berg's rank," she said. "His name is Xaphan—the fallen angel who keeps the fires of hell burning at full blast."

"You got that right," he said, and decided to tell her all about Baron von Berg's lost submarine and the *Flammenschwert*.

She looked stunned, as if everything made sense to her now. "I know the legend of Greek fire and its use during the Crusades, but I never imagined that the Nazis had found a way to tap Atlantean technology."

"Apparently, they did. I've seen the technology up close and personal."

He could see she was lost in thought when something like a flash of lightning flickered across her soft brown eyes. "And what about Baron von Berg's safe deposit box in Bern?" she asked. "What did you find inside?"

"This," he said, and slapped down the Shekel of Tyre on the table. "See, I've got one, too."

31

Serena stared at the coin on the table and fully grasped Midas's predicament and her own. Midas had been claiming some sort of provisional status within the Thirty based on his control over Baron von Berg's box, with the assumption that somehow, someday, he would possess its contents. Now Conrad had the coin and, technically, membership in the Alignment.

Until somebody like Midas or herself killed him for it.

"How did you get this?" she asked. "And why couldn't Midas?"

Conrad explained the code in the metal plate from Baron von Berg's skull, the self-destruct box in Bern, and how he'd circumvented all the security and escaped. He smiled and said, "So I guess we're going to Rhodes."

Serena was shaking inside. "I don't think so, Conrad."

"Names and faces, Serena. Names and faces. And, I'll bet you, the designated target for the *Flammenschwert.*"

She couldn't let it happen, she realized. But she didn't want to fight him now. "We'll need a plan," she said. "A good one."

"How about this one?" he said, and produced a long tube he had been keeping under the table. It was a roll file, and inside were architectural drawings of a massive fortress. He spread them across the table. "Look familiar?"

"The Palace of the Grandmaster," she said. "Where did you get these?"

"Beneath the floorboards in the Magnolia Suite of the main villa."

"Seriously, Conrad."

"Seriously," he told her. "This was the last residence of Mussolini before he was executed. Rhodes belonged to the Italians back then, and Il Duce had grand plans for his Palace of the Grandmaster."

"It wasn't his," Serena said. "It was built by the Knights of St. John of Jerusalem in the seventh century."

"True, but that palace was pretty much demolished by the explosion of Turkish gunpowder centuries later. Mussolini restored and modified it between 1937 and 1940. These are the plans of the architect Vittorio Mesturino."

Serena didn't like the direction of this conversation and had to change it, put Conrad back on his heels. "How could you possibly know there were blueprints beneath the floorboards in the Magnolia Suite?"

"I didn't," he said. "But the hotel staff told me that was the suite Mussolini slept in, and I knew from his other residences where he liked to hide documents."

"Everybody missed it during the hotel's renovation?"

"The beauty of preservation," he explained. "The charm of this place is that most everything is as it was. Now look at the blueprint. There's a secret council chamber under the palace that's not shown in any contemporary floor plans. It's directly beneath the large courtyard in the center of the palace. That's where the Knights of the Alignment are going to meet."

Serena stared at the blueprint and then looked up at Conrad, who was studying the schematics and clearly making plans in his head. Yet again his genius genuinely frightened her. She was a careful strategist, but Conrad was opportunistic to a fault, able to find an opening when all doors seemed closed and bullets were raining down. That wasn't going to save him on Rhodes, though. Nothing would, if he actually stepped foot on the island.

"I think we should look it over after dessert," she said. "I'm going to shower and change first. It's been a very long day, and the week ahead is looking longer still."

She excused herself and walked into the boathouse. It was lavishly appointed, and she half believed she was capable of going to bed with Conrad that night. It could be their last chance ever. She picked up her backpack from the bed and went into the marble bathroom with flower petals everywhere. She splashed water on her face, feeling the queasiness of betrayal.

She pulled out her Vertu phone from her backpack and placed a call. The voice on the other end said, "Well?"

"I've got him," she said. "He's yours."

32

Conrad sat on the bed, anxiously waiting for Serena to emerge from the bathroom and wondering exactly what he'd see. There wasn't a lot of room in her little backpack for a change of clothes or a nightgown. But in every previous do-or-die moment of physical intimacy between them, she'd always managed to surprise him and leave him wanting.

"Conrad?" she called from the bathroom. "How did you find out which box was von Berg's?"

"It was etched beneath the metal plate in his skull."

"What was the code?"

"ARES, the god of war."

"Makes sense," she called out. "And the box number?"

"1740."

There was no response.

Conrad paused, wondering if he should say anything. Then he looked up to see Serena step out of the bathroom wearing only his white dress shirt, which managed to both hide and highlight her irresistible figure. He swallowed hard and stood up as she approached him.

She stood barely an inch away from his face, looking up at him. Their bodies did not touch, but he felt an unmistakable exchange of sexual energy between them.

"Do you really think it's a weapon forged from the technology of Atlantis?" she asked.

"I think it really turns water to fire on some molecular level, and that von Berg had a connection to Antarctica, which might have a connection with Atlantis."

"You're the one with the DNA of angels, Conrad. The Alignment and Americans both think you've got traces of Nephilim blood."

The Nephilim, according to the sixth chapter of Genesis, were the offspring of the mysterious "sons of God"—fallen angels, according to some theologians—who bred with women. Their civilization was wiped off the face of the earth by the Great Flood, which the Bible said was God's wrath upon a corrupted humanity.

"You say Nephilim and I say Atlantean," Conrad said. "But at the end of the day, we all share the same ancestral DNA."

"Some more than others."

Conrad shrugged. "Hasn't helped me yet."

"But it helped me back in D.C.," she reminded him. "Your blood provided the vaccine that saved me from the Alignment's military-grade flu virus."

"Oh, right," he said. "We've already swapped bodily fluids."

Serena's warm gaze embraced him even as she maintained her one-inch distance. It was all Conrad could do to keep from grabbing her.

"Why did you come back, Conrad?" she asked him. "After what I did to you?"

"I knew there were other forces at work, Serena," he told her. "I had to find out what they were."

Her face looked sad, defeated. "And then what?" she pressed him. "What were your plans for our future—if we had one?"

"You mean if you weren't a member of the Alignment? Or a nun?"

"Technically, I'm not a nun. I had to give up my role with the Carmelites for the Dei. And since the Dei doesn't recognize women as such, I'm pretty much a lay leader in the Church."

Conrad felt a glimmer of hope. "That's wonderful," he blurted, grasping her hand. "The best news yet."

"So how many children do you want, Conrad?" she asked, obviously trying to scare him. She was no wallflower. "You'll have to take care of them, you know."

"Me?" he asked.

"Just because I'm not a nun doesn't mean I'll be giving up the Lord's work traveling to the farthest corners of the earth to help the helpless."

"Okay with me," he said, playing along. "The ruins I explore tend to be in the same places. You can just strap the little guys to your back and swing from trees all you want."

"What's wrong with little girls, Conrad?"

"Nothing," he said. "But biologically, aren't I the one to decide that? Guess there's only one way to find out." He gently pulled her closer to him, and his voice turned tender. "You're the only thing I have to show for my life, Serena. Everything else is dust. That

Hebrew slave settlement I found by the pyramids in Giza. Gone. Atlantis in Antarctica. Gone. The only thing I ever recovered were the globes, and you and Uncle Sam stole them from me."

"I'm so sorry, Conrad. I really am."

"No, you don't understand, Serena. I'm okay with it. I don't need to make any great discoveries. We can make our own. You're what I've been searching for all my life. I knew it the moment I saw you. And I don't ever want to lose you."

Her eyes sparkled with tears. She threw her arms around his neck and turned her lovely mouth up to his and kissed him.

His whole body and spirit seemed to come alive as they embraced. He couldn't believe this was about to happen.

"Please forgive me, Conrad, for all I've done to you," she said, kissing him again. "For what I'm going to do to you."

His head was swimming in ecstasy. Or was it something else? He opened his eyes and saw the room spinning behind Serena's blurred face.

"I hate you," he groaned as whatever drug she had applied to her lips took hold of his body.

"Forgive me," she whispered as she kissed him generously, passionately, until he blacked out.

33

1740!" Conrad shouted, and bolted upright in bed.

He opened his eyes. He was inside an Airstream trailer with a loud but familiar hum around him. The air was cold, and there was a woman sitting next to him, but it wasn't Serena. It was Wanda Randolph, the former U.S. Capitol Police officer who had taken shots at him in the tunnels beneath the U.S. Capitol.

"Where am I?" he asked.

"You're on U.S. soil now, so to speak," she said, and smiled. "Everything's okay."

He looked at the wires and electrodes attached to his body. "The hell it is," he said, and with his right arm struck Wanda in the head and knocked her against the Airstream's wall. He pulled off the wires, opened the trailer door, ran out into a cavernous hangar, and looked for an exit.

"Stop!" Wanda shouted, running up behind with a gun pointed at him.

He ran past a chopper and a tank to a large door and found the button to open it. Warning lights flashed and an alarm sounded. As the door slowly opened from the top down, Conrad realized where he was even before he saw the curvature of the Mediterranean Sea thirty thousand feet below.

There were more shouts and the thunder of boots on the metal flooring, and Conrad turned to see a team of U.S. airmen surround him with their guns drawn.

"Step away from the panel, sir," an airman ordered.

Conrad knew he was going nowhere and stepped away.

The airmen holstered their guns and closed the door as Wanda escorted him back to the Airstream trailer, where Marshall Packard was waiting with some files.

"Good, you're up," Packard said.

"Where's Serena?" Conrad demanded.

"On her way to Rhodes," Packard said. "She exchanged you for our celestial globe. She was actually going to attempt to slip a forgery past the Alignment, which never would have worked. Now she can deliver the goods at the EU summit and be our eyes and ears inside the Alignment."

Conrad shook his head. "You don't need me, Packard. Why did you do it?"

"Your girl said she needed you off the playing field to convince the Alignment you're dead, like she promised, and she had some bizarre notion that you might not play along," Packard said. "So we'll keep an eye on you."

"Not a chance," said Conrad. "You know she's dead meat once she turns over those globes."

"That's a risk she's willing to take to identify the remaining officers of the Alignment. Meanwhile, we've already seen both globes and know what the Alignment is getting. So there's no downside for us."

"You're idiots," Conrad said. "The globes work together. You have no idea what the Alignment has."

"Enlighten me."

"The number of Baron von Berg's safe deposit box was for the date 1740."

"Yeah, yeah, we're ahead of you, son," Packard said. "The only thing that popped up in history for that year was the death in Rome of Pope Clement XII, who had forbidden Roman Catholics from belonging to Masonic lodges on pain of excommunication. Von Berg's joke. Ha, ha."

"Joke's on you, Packard. That was also the year that the Masons in Berlin established the Royal Mother Lodge of the Three Globes. I don't know why I didn't see it before. I guess I needed Baron von Berg and his box number to finally make the connection."

The color drained from Packard's face. "Three globes?"

"That's right," Conrad said. "There were three of them all along. The Masons must have kept one in Europe and let the other two go to the New World. How much you want to bet that the Alignment has had the third globe all along? Now Serena is about to hand them the other two."

"But for what purpose?" Packard demanded. "What the hell do three globes do that two globes can't?"

"Reveal the target and timetable for detonating the *Flammenschwert*, that's what," Conrad said.

PART THREE
Rhodes

34

The early-morning sun glinted off the calm waters of Mandraki Harbor as Midas's yacht, the *Mercedes*, motored past the long breakwater with its three windmills toward the medieval city of Rhodes. There, atop its highest point, its massive fortress walls dwarfing the city below, was the Palace of the Grandmaster.

At least the *Mercedes* could enjoy the intimacy of the harbor with its pleasure craft and seaside cafés, Midas thought as they entered the mouth of the harbor. The *Midas* would have required them to anchor farther away.

Much smaller than the *Midas*, the *Mercedes* was a mere 250-footer that he picked up in Cyprus the day after Mercedes's funeral in Paris. He had planned to arrive in Rhodes in the *Midas*. It had taken two days to acquire a yacht large enough to take in a submersible. Midas had contacted his rogue submersible that had been roaming the deep with the *Flammenschwert* all this time. As soon as the captain emerged after five days underwater, Midas rewarded him with a bullet to the brain and dumped him overboard.

Now the *Mercedes* passed between the two defensive stone towers where the Colossus of Rhodes was said to have straddled the harbor. The giant statue had been one of the seven wonders of the ancient world before an earthquake in 226 B.C. brought it down into the sea a century after it was erected.

Midas left the deck and entered his stateroom to admire the magnificent sculpture in the center of the room—a bust of Aphrodite, the ancient Greek goddess of love. The cover was brilliant. As an act of goodwill, Midas would be returning to the Greeks the bronze head of Aphrodite from the British Museum, which he had managed to exchange for several works of art he had purchased at auction from Sotheby's on Bond Street. It had taken months of negotiations with the museum's Department of Greek and Roman Antiquities, but he needed this particular bust to both house the warhead and bring as a gift for the Greeks at the summit.

The beauty of the head of Aphrodite was that it was a sculptural mask of the Greek goddess of love, so the back was missing. That enabled Midas to fit the *Flammenschwert* warhead neatly inside. The fitted plaster piece on the back of the mask would be tossed once the transfer of the warhead had been made, and the mask could be handed off to the Greeks for display in the exhibition halls of the palace.

Midas ran his finger down the face of the serene mask. The deeply set eyes had come from a complete statue and dated back to the second or first century B.C. It was seventeen inches high, twelve inches wide, and eleven inches deep. The warhead was only six inches in diameter, inside of which were two pounds of

Semtex plastic explosive and an initiator device. The detonator would explode the Semtex and ignite the metallic fire pellets of the *Flammenschwert*. The fire pellets, in turn, would ignite any water around it.

Midas looked at his watch. He was due to deliver the mask to the Palace of the Grandmaster in twenty minutes.

Vadim was waiting on the dock with the limousine and a police motorcycle escort. They placed the packing crate with the Aphrodite mask in the back and then made their way to the palace.

"Where's the bitch?" Midas asked.

"At the convention center," Vadim said.

Midas sighed. He felt vulnerable without his membership coin. His deal with the Alignment had been that he would recover Baron von Berg's coin and the *Flammenschwert* from the baron's sub in exchange for a seat on the Council of Thirty. But then Conrad Yeats had ruined everything. Fortunately, Yeats was out of the picture now, and the coin would soon be in Midas's hands.

They drove along the harbor toward the Old City. The medieval town of Rhodes was surrounded and defined by a triple circuit of walls, which looked to Midas to be in very good condition. The fortress city seemed to have it all: moats, towers, bridges, and seven gates.

Vadim pulled the limousine up to the security checkpoint at the Eleftherias Gate, or the Gate of Liberty. Only permanent residents of the Old City were allowed to drive on the narrow cobblestone streets. But today dignitaries were allowed through with a police escort.

They followed the stone-paved streets past the third-century temple of Aphrodite and turned onto the main drag, the Odos Ippoton, or the Street of Knights, named for the Knights of St. John, who had established themselves on the island in the fourteenth century and who Midas was convinced must have been a front for the Alignment at one point. At the entrance was the fifteenth-century Knights Hospital, and at the end of the street, opposite the Church of St. John, stood the imposing Palace of the Grandmaster with its spherical towers.

They drove past the massive round towers flanking the main entrance to the palace—where Greek *Evzones* in uniform stood on either side of the sharp arch—and went around to the west entrance by the square tower, where a Greek cultural attaché welcomed Midas and the Aphrodite mask into the grand reception hall. This was the regal backdrop where the opening and closing ceremonies were staged for the cameras, while the sessions and breakout panels took place in the ballrooms, conference centers, and suites at the Rodos Palace hotel and international convention center ten minutes away.

"On behalf of the people of Greece, I thank you for returning to us the Aphrodite head from the British Museum," the attaché said.

"It is my pleasure," Midas said. "And I was told I could spend a moment alone with my dear Aphrodite before I handed it over."

"Yes," said the attaché. An armed Greek *Evzone* with an earpiece appeared and led Midas past a Medusa mosaic down a large vaulted corridor. There were 158 rooms in the palace, all bedecked with antique furniture, exquisite polychrome marbles, sculptures, and icons. Only twenty-four of those rooms were open to the public on any given day.

But the room to which Midas was escorted wasn't in any of the tourist guides or public blueprints registered with Greece; it was even closed to the VIPs of the summit. It was a chamber constructed beneath the palace. Closed to all but members of the Alignment, it was known as the Hall of Knights council room.

Midas entered the hall and waited for his escort to leave. Then a door slid open, and he walked into the adjoining chamber with the Aphrodite mask, prepared to hand the *Flammenschwert* to Uriel.

But Uriel wasn't there—only a single copper globe, split open, resting on a stand on top of a large round table. Inside the globe was an envelope, and next to the round table was a fireplace with a fire burning.

No surprise here, really. Midas had known the identity of Uriel, and vice versa, all along. They weren't supposed to be seen together in public, a rule Midas had violated at the disastrous Bilderberg party. But as this handoff was private, he hadn't been sure what to expect.

He looked at the globe. It was the first time he had seen one of them.

So this is the delivery device.

Not a missile. Not a warplane. But this old globe.

If it had been his choice, Midas would have held on to the *Flammenschwert* until its detonation. He certainly wouldn't have left it alone here. But the holier-than-thou Uriel didn't want to see the *Flammenschwert,* much less touch it. And Uriel was the only one who could get it into position and leave the dirty work of pulling the trigger to Midas.

He opened the envelope, read the handwritten note, tossed it into the fireplace, and watched it burn to ashes.

He removed the plaster back of the bronze Aphrodite mask and tossed it into the fireplace, too. Then he put his hand behind the sphere containing the *Flammenschwert* and turned the mask over until the sphere rested heavily in his hand. He lifted the mask with the other hand and placed it on the table. With both hands, he carefully placed the sphere containing the *Flammenschwert* inside the globe, where it fit snugly. He sealed the globe shut like a skin over the warhead sphere. The seam along the 40th parallel seemed to disappear.

The door on the other side of the chamber magically opened. He picked up Aphrodite's head, brushed it off, and walked out.

35

Conrad watched another F-16 take off from the tarmac and walked back up the rear ramp of the C-17 to Packard's office inside the "silver bullet." Packard had been on the phone ever since they'd landed on Crete. The Greek air base was home to the Hellenic Air Force's 115th Combat Wing, but the U.S. Naval Support Activity Souda Bay occupied over a hundred acres on the north side to support Sixth Fleet operations in the eastern Mediterranean and Middle East. Conrad was waiting to hear if he would get any of that support now.

Packard, still on the phone, frowned at him and slid across his desk the leather binder containing Conrad's hastily prepared but well-documented report on the Three Globes Society and their relationship to the Freemasons of colonial America, the Nazis, and the contemporary Alignment. Conrad picked up the binder and saw Packard's notations in the margins. The most frequent words were "insane," "crazy," "speculation," and "aha." There were no comments on Conrad's outline of possible origins of the globes and whether they were originally housed in King Solomon's Temple, or perhaps some place older still.

Packard hung up the phone and looked at him. "It's going to take a few hours, but I think we can clear you with Interpol so that police everywhere will stop shooting at you on sight."

"You can't do that," Conrad said. "Midas would know that Serena lied to him about my demise. That alone would put her loyalty in doubt with the Alignment. I need an alias with ID to get me through all zones of security."

Packard sighed. "That's going to make it easier to nab the globes?"

"I don't need to steal anything. That's the beauty of it. I just need to see the three globes for myself. In and out."

"Because you think they'll reveal where and possibly when the Alignment will detonate the *Flammenschwert*?" Packard asked skeptically. "I'm not sure I'm ready to make that assumption."

Conrad said, "I think the leadership of the Alignment will use the message of the globes as some sort of mystical directive for their mystical weapon, even if they manipulate the meaning to suit their ends. So that message is invaluable regardless."

"Serena's whip-smart, son. What makes you think she can't figure it out for herself?"

"Not on the spot, she can't. She hasn't had the time I've had with both globes. And she's a linguist, not an astro-archaeologist. She won't be able to figure out the celestial-terrestrial alignments between the globes, let alone translate them to real-world coordinates. Even if she could, you know they're not going to let her leave

Rhodes alive once she's delivered the only leverage she's ever had with the Alignment."

Packard licked a finger and flipped through the report again, clearly still agitated with himself and his analysts for having missed the possibility of the existence of a third globe. "So let me get this straight: You think all three used to be in Solomon's Temple and were later buried beneath the Temple Mount when the Babylonians destroyed the First Temple. Furthermore, you think they may have been the Holy Grail that the Knights Templar were after when they started digging up the Temple Mount looking for Solomon's treasures during the Crusades."

"I think they worked to pinpoint a location of some great treasure, but it may not have been gold."

"Then what the hell else could it have been? And don't tell me the Ark of the Covenant."

"Obviously, something of great value. In ancient Egypt and Tiahuanaco and Atlantis, that meant the secrets of First Time or the End Times."

"The Alignment already has the secret of the End Times, son, and it's called the *Flammenschwert*. That's how they're going to end things for all of us. And that's why we need to find that weapon." Packard's face reddened, and he threw the report down. "I traded the globe for you and got nothing."

There was something just a little too forced in Packard's voice, and Conrad suddenly understood.

"You bastard," he said. "You weren't that desperate to get me. You just wanted to give Serena the globe and make her think she worked for it. What did you do to it?"

Packard sighed. "It's got a tracker."

Conrad slapped his hand on the table, furious. "Like the Alignment's not going to find it and kill her? Then they'll have the globes as well as the *Flammenschwert,* and you'll still have nothing."

"I told you, son, she's our girl at this EU summit. Both she and Midas are invited. You and Uncle Sam aren't. Security is going to be extremely tight, and the Alignment is supposed to think you're dead. Anybody recognizes you, she's dead."

"She's dead already."

Packard seemed to be going back and forth in his head, weighing the risks and rewards. "Well, I can't send U.S. troops, even Randolph, into this theater," he said, as if thinking aloud. "And when it comes to European summits, trust me, it's always theater."

"So I'm in."

"Hey, it's your head and hers," Packard said. "This doesn't come back to Uncle Sam. Just stay out of sight, if that's possible, and report as soon as you know anything."

"I told you, I can do this without being seen, even by Serena. But I'll be watching her."

"As will everybody else. So watch yourself."

Ten minutes later, the twin engines and four blades of the Super Puma Eurocopter were winding up for takeoff as Wanda Randolph walked Conrad across the tarmac and gave him his identification badges.

"Your name is Firat Kayda, a military liaison with us in Turkey, and you're working the EU summit for the delegation from Ankara. It'll take you about an hour in the air from here to there."

Conrad looked at the four Greek airmen in the chopper. They already seemed to be glaring at him, the Turk. "Packard is truly determined to make everybody in this world hate me, isn't he?"

"Well, he tries," said Wanda. "At least this way, the Greeks won't be asking you too many questions on the way over."

36

Serena stepped off her seaplane in Mandraki Harbor at Rhodes and felt like she had stepped back in time to the Crusades. The Palace of the Grandmaster, the fifteenth-century Tower of St. Nicholas, and the Mosque of Sultan completely overwhelmed the contemporary seaside cafés, chic shops, and sleek yachts lining the harbor.

Brother Lorenzo of the Dei, his mouth agape in astonishment, was waiting for her by a silver Mercedes-Benz G55 AMG sport-utility vehicle as she walked toward him, holding the celestial globe from the Americans against her belly and looking like a pregnant woman about to give birth.

She felt naked without the full escort of Swiss Guards she normally had at her disposal. But this was not official Vatican business, and if any agents of the Alignment were watching from rooftops through scopes, it was probably for her protection until she delivered the globes. There was no reason for any sort of smash-and-grab attack.

"The genuine celestial globe," Lorenzo said reverently as he helped her load it into the back. He had no clue where she had gone between Paris and Rhodes and was clearly impressed with her acquisition. "But how?"

She certainly wasn't going to tell him. "Where's Benito?"

"At the convention center with the terrestrial globe and the fake celestial globe."

"Let's go, then."

The Rodos Palace hotel and convention center sat on a hill overlooking Ialyssos Bay and billed itself as Greece's finest and largest convention resort, specially built to host the European heads of state. Serena could see from all the armored vehicles and police outside that this was certainly the case today. Some twenty-seven ministers of the European nations and all their security had descended on the peace summit to discuss and possibly reach some sort of international resolution on the fate of Jerusalem, which they had deemed the key to establishing an independent Palestinian state and peace in the Middle East.

Lorenzo bypassed the main entrance to the complex on Trianton Avenue and rounded the corner to the vehicle inspection point in front of the drop-off lane at the VIP entrance. He popped the rear hatch, lowered his window, and handed to a police officer his license and registration, along with their summit ID badges. Serena watched the officer slide the badges through a card reader while four soldiers surrounded the SUV and passed mirrors under the chassis in search of explosives.

A couple of the soldiers had gathered around the globe and

asked that she and Lorenzo step out and explain while the interior cabin of the SUV could be examined.

"It's part of the art for one of the exhibitions at the summit," she said. "We're not even taking it inside. We're picking up another globe at the loading dock outside the Jupiter Ballroom and then taking both of them to the Palace of the Grandmaster for viewing."

"Of course, Sister Serghetti," the officer said. "I am sorry for the inconvenience."

She climbed back inside the SUV, and Lorenzo got behind the wheel and started it up again. Then he drove them all of fifty yards down to the loading entrance outside the Jupiter Ballroom.

In the ballroom, Serena found the EU heads of state seated in front of their national flags around a pentagon of tables beneath Murano crystal chandeliers. Around the leaders was a much larger ring of tables packed with diplomatic staff, international press, and banks of equipment for audiovisual and simultaneous interpretation.

She made her way behind the press area, glancing up now and then to see the image of a talking head flash across the large screen over the stage. She could only guess how many of those faces belonged to the Thirty. Whoever her counterparts of the Alignment turned out to be, Serena was convinced that the message of the Templar globes and this EU summit were connected symbiotically. The origins of the globes had been traced to King Solomon's Temple in Jerusalem, after all, and it was the future of that city under discussion in this ballroom.

She found Benito backstage with the globes, which were disregarded by all the technical people moving to and fro as mere set pieces and part of the show, somebody else's responsibility.

Midas was there, too, and he wasted no time. "You have something for me?"

Serena removed the Shekel of Tyre from her pocket and handed it to him.

He didn't take her word for it and took out some sort of pocket-sized device to shine an infrared light on it. "The ancients used some kind of polymer material on the coins. The effect is like an invisible UV stamp. See?" he said. He showed her the coin under the light, and to her amazement, she saw four arrowlike markers emblazoned at the cardinal points around the bust of Baal. They made a cross, and she recognized it as the adopted flag of the island's Knights of St. John.

Midas held up his infrared device and said accusingly, "I used this on your celestial globe here, too. It's a fake."

"I have the real one in my car outside. You were to give me further instructions?"

Midas seemed pleased. "You are to take the globes to the west entrance of the Palace of the Grandmaster at three o'clock, where you will be met by a nameless Greek attaché and directed to a chamber where you will present the globes to Uriel," he told her. "You have ten minutes."

She left Lorenzo and the faux celestial globe at the convention center and climbed into the back of the SUV with the two genuine globes. Benito pulled onto the access drive, and the police waved them through the exit gate.

Uriel, she thought. Serena had never heard that name among the Thirty. But she knew that Uriel was the name of the angel in Genesis who guarded the gate to the Garden of Eden with a flaming sword after God kicked Adam and Eve out of paradise. Conrad's information about the *Flammenschwert* weapon was beginning to make sense, and she was eager to find out who this Uriel could be.

As they drove toward the Palace of the Grandmaster, she could tell Benito was impressed with her acquisition of the genuine celestial globe but concerned all the same.

"And *Signor* Yeats?" he asked, glancing at her in the rearview mirror.

"With the Americans," she answered.

Benito bit his tongue, but Serena could read his eyes: *That man will hate you for the rest of your life, you cold, heartless bitch.* Well, he wouldn't say that. Benito didn't swear, and he knew more than anybody else what was necessary. He seemed sad all the same, though.

But she had come to Rhodes to unmask the Alignment. In a few minutes she would deliver the globes, as promised. In a few hours she would attend tonight's Council Meeting of the Thirty. Then everything she had worked for and sacrificed—including a life with Conrad—would pay off once and for all.

37

The Greek pilot brought the Super Puma Eurocopter over Rhodes at nine hundred feet, steering clear of the EU summit's security red zones below and following an alternative glide path to the airstrip. The skies were clear and offered Conrad a spectacular view of the island below.

"Security zones?" Conrad asked in broken English with the best Turkish accent he could make up. His attempt was so bad it actually worked, cracking up one of the Greeks. Another, named Koulos, decided to help the confused Turk get a lay of the land.

"The red inner-security zones are around the Palace of the Grandmaster in the Old Town down there, and the Rodos Palace hotel and convention center are in New Town over there," Koulos shouted in English above the whir of the rotor blades. "They are linked by the harbor drive. Only authorized personnel or security assigned to those zones can pass through the checkpoints."

Conrad nodded.

"The walls of Old Town outside the Palace of the Grandmaster are the perimeter of the yellow outer-security zone. No vehicles without proper registration and full inspection are allowed through the gates."

Conrad pulled out the military BlackBerry Packard had given him with the GPS tracking program. He called up the satellite map of Rhodes from Google Earth and tried to find the pulsing blue dot that represented the celestial globe Packard had given Serena. The glare from the sun outside the chopper windows made it too difficult to read the screen until they landed and he jumped off onto the tarmac.

That was when he got the fix: The globe was in the red zone at the convention center, hopefully with the other two.

Conrad signed for his police motorcycle as Firat Kayda. Though the bike belonged to the police department, it wasn't an official police motorcycle and had no siren. When he reached the convention center, his ID badge worked beautifully, and he was able to glide through the checkpoint to the main entrance of the hotel, allegedly to meet his Turkish superiors.

He followed the GPS signal through the hotel atrium and into the airy exhibition area where all kinds of "green" technology companies promised to turn the Middle East into a tropical paradise for investment and generate fat profits to European investors. "More than oil" seemed to be the theme, highlighting the commercial benefits of peace in the region.

The bright sunlight provided him with the perfect excuse to keep his sunglasses on, like many others, and look nondescript as he passed a spectacular circular staircase toward the Delphi Amphitheater.

He stopped outside the door and put away his BlackBerry. The security guard glanced at his badge and nodded.

Conrad slipped into the back of the three-level amphitheater, which was packed with almost six hundred delegates. Up on the stage, speaking from the podium before an impressive array of flat-panel screens flashing all sorts of logos and graphics, was Roman Midas.

What does he have to say that any of these people want to hear? Conrad unconsciously shrank back against the wall with a group of bystanders who couldn't find seats. He felt like a convict in a police lineup for Midas to pick out. But all the lights and attention were on Midas now, and Conrad doubted the man could see anyone beyond the front row.

"It's the new alchemy," Midas proclaimed. "Water springing forth from the desert."

High-definition graphics showed how the same deep-mining technology that Midas Minerals & Mining had used to extract oil from the "world's most difficult to reach substrata" could now be harnessed to extract water from the hidden rivers and aquifers of the Sinai Peninsula.

Midas said, "The dust bowl becomes the bread basket of the Middle East, freeing the region from dependence on foreign agriculture and offering local populations the opportunity to grow and export more than oil."

The names of various Israeli and Arab partners popped up on the screens to underscore the international cooperation of this "consortium of leading industries" to "rid the Middle East of its dependence on oil."

Well, that's a new one, Conrad thought as he slowly made his way along the curving back wall of the room. He suspected he would come upon a door leading to a projection booth or control room of some kind, which was probably as obscure a place as any to store the globes until they could be moved. He couldn't imagine them alone without armed security. But the only door that appeared was the other rear exit.

He stepped out of the amphitheater into the bar reception area and saw the celestial globe standing there like some piece of art with a young man in a suit and collar—a priest's collar.

Worse, the priest had recognized him.

Damn, Conrad thought as he marched up to the priest.

The priest began, "Dr. Yeats—"

"Shut up," Conrad said quietly, and glanced around. "What the hell is going on?"

"You needn't worry," the priest said drily. "This isn't the globe you gave her. This is a fake. She took the real one with her after she removed the tracker and put it inside this one."

"Where is she . . . Lorenzo?" Conrad said, reading the priest's ID badge.

Lorenzo had suddenly taken a vow of silence.

Conrad pressed him. "She's in danger."

The priest screwed up his eyes at Conrad. "From whom?"

"Last time, Lorenzo."

"She's at her three o'clock appointment," Lorenzo said. "Do I need to call security?"

"No, but I'm taking this." Conrad took the globe off its pedestal and walked off with it, leaving an open-mouthed Lorenzo behind.

Outside, Conrad opened the globe, tossed the tracker, and strapped the globe to the back of his motorcycle. Then he pulled out his BlackBerry and called Wanda Randolph.

"Report," said Wanda.

"Tell Packard she found the tracker. But she's still with the packages. I need you to hack the security system here and see when was the last time her ID badge was scanned."

"Copy that," Wanda said.

Conrad looked at his watch. It was 3:05. He was worried he was too late.

Wanda rang him back two minutes later. "She passed through the checkpoint at Liberty Gate in the Old Town. She's going to the Palace of the Grandmaster with two packages. They're listed only as 'art' on the system."

But Conrad had hung up at "Grandmaster," kick-started his bike, and roared off toward the fortress.

38

Back at the hotel and convention center, Lorenzo crossed the atrium lobby and approached the commanding officer at the security desk. He was an ambitious priest, and Dr. Yeats had given him a golden opportunity to accelerate his rise within the Dei even as he attempted to protect his superiors.

"I just saw the fugitive who murdered Mercedes Le Roche," Lorenzo said breathlessly. "Conrad Yeats the American. He is here at the summit."

The Greek looked at Lorenzo's badge and collar and decided to take the report seriously enough to ask further questions. "Was he wearing a badge, Father?"

"Yes," said Lorenzo helpfully. "The name was Firat Kayda, and it had a red security stripe for access to the inner zones. Holy Mother of God, maybe this American killed Kayda and has taken his place to kill someone here!"

"Please, Father. Do not repeat this. We will investigate."

Lorenzo detected a dismissive tone in the Greek official's voice. "You're not going to do any such thing, are you?"

The officer picked up a phone. "Firat Kayda," he said, and hung up.

"That's all?" Lorenzo said.

"Please wait, Father."

The officer attended to some papers with the other officers while Lorenzo watched, burning with anger. A minute later, the Greek saw his frown and looked at a computer terminal. "Here it is," he said, looking at a time-stamped video clip of the moment Kayda had passed through the hotel checkpoint. A concerned expression took hold on the Greek's face as the facial-recognition program kicked in. "There is a high degree of probability that you are correct."

"At last," Lorenzo said.

The Greek started typing furiously. "I am flagging his name and attaching the video for when he presents himself at a checkpoint. He'll be refused entry and arrested immediately."

"Don't forget that he is armed and dangerous, Officer. He has killed and may kill again."

The Greek looked up warily. "Thank you very much, Father. You have been most helpful."

Lorenzo made the sign of the cross and walked away.

39

Vadim was sitting inside the Peugeot parked opposite the Palace of the Grandmaster. He looked past the vehicle ID badge dangling from his rearview mirror to see the silver Mercedes SUV drive through.

He reached back and pulled down the rear seat to access the trunk. Squirming next to the blocks of C4 plastic explosives was a bound, gagged, and badly beaten Abdil Zawas. Vadim had brought the Egyptian to Rhodes directly from Bern hours before the security checkpoints had been set up. Since this car had been registered to a resident for several years, the security forces sweeping the Old Town yellow zone hadn't opened its trunk.

Abdil was waking up a little sooner than Vadim wanted. The streets were so narrow and cars so few that he couldn't afford to have somebody walk by while Abdil banged his head and feet to draw attention.

"Siesta isn't over," Vadim said, and removed an injection pen from his pocket. "We have to keep you alive long enough for the coroner to pronounce your proper cause of death as a martyr for Allah." He delighted at the look of horror in Abdil's eyes. The pen was filled only with a concentrated dose of trazodone to put him to sleep. Nothing painful, unfortunately, and it was a shame to think that the Egyptian wouldn't be awake for his final moments.

"Don't you wonder how many of your little sluts will miss you when you're gone?" Vadim asked, injecting the trazodone into Abdil's thick neck. "I think you'll miss them more where you're going."

Abdil's eyes rolled around in panic even as his eyelids grew heavy. In a few minutes it would all be over for the late, great Abdil Zawas.

"I'm going to make you famous, Abdil," Vadim told the Egyptian. "You're about to open a new front on the war against Jews and Crusaders. Look at this clip that's about to be posted on YouTube. Recognize yourself?"

Vadim was about to play the video on his BlackBerry when the device began to ring. It was Midas.

"Security says Yeats is alive and on Rhodes," Midas barked. "She has betrayed the Alignment."

"You seem surprised," Vadim said. "Your plan was always to kill her as soon as she delivered the globes. She knows too much. More than I do. Nothing has changed. Yeats won't make it in time to interfere."

"Is everything set?"

"Yes," Vadim said. "The only street into or out of the Palace of the Grandmaster is the Street of Knights. I'll take care of her as soon as she leaves the palace."

"She must not have even a moment to contact anybody with information about what she may have learned from Uriel or figured out for herself," Midas said, and then there was a pause. "Remember, Vadim. She will be the second car. I repeat: the second car. Not the first. Everything is lost if you mistake the two."

Vadim said, "I won't."

"See that you don't," Midas said. "It must look like the first car was the target but that Zawas hit Serghetti's car instead and blew himself up in the process."

"Yes," said Vadim, looking at Abdil's limp body in the mirror. "I understand."

40

All the way down the Street of Knights toward the Palace of the Grandmaster, Serena wondered who Uriel could possibly be. If his role within the Alignment was true to his name, then Uriel could be the one who ultimately possessed the *Flammenschwert*. That pointed to Midas, however, and she braced herself to see his ugly smile waiting for her with the third globe.

"I wish I could join you inside, *signorina*," Benito said as he pulled the G55 SUV up to the west tower entrance.

"Me, too," she said.

The Greek attaché Midas had told her about was already waiting with two aides and a cart. Benito opened the rear door, and the aides placed the two steel boxes containing the copper globes on the cart. Serena followed through the entrance.

Inside, they walked past the Medusa mosaic and down a large vaulted corridor to the lower level. It was right out of the blueprints Conrad had shown her back at the lake in Italy. And when they entered the Hall of Knights and left her alone with the globes, nobody had to tell her what room she stood in. Its scale and decor announced itself in a sinister way.

Then the small wooden door on the side opened by itself, and she saw the adjoining chamber and the reflection of a fire bouncing off what could only be the third globe. She pushed the cart inside, next to the round table, and beheld the globe on top.

The third globe.

She stood in silence, staring at it. It was magnificent, like something forged from the depths of a volcano or the mountain copper ore of Atlantis. It closely resembled its celestial and terrestrial cousins and was clearly part of the family. But the dials carved across the surface of this globe marked it as an armillary, built to predict the cycles of the sun, moon, and planets. It was the third element of time that Brother Lorenzo had correctly suspected was missing from their calculations back at the Vatican.

The door opened, and she looked up to see General Gellar, the Israeli defense minister, looking her up and down in surprise.

The feeling is mutual, she thought. "You're Uriel?" They had been acquaintances for quite some time, and suddenly, they both looked at each other in a very different way. "What do you want with these globes?" she asked.

"You have to ask?" Gellar sounded offended. "They're ours. They belong to Israel. You took them."

"We took them?"

"The Knights Templar stole them from under the Temple Mount along with whatever else they could pillage to fund their wars, increase their powers, and persecute the Jews."

Serena took it in, trying to figure this all out. "Well, on behalf of the Roman Catholic Church, I certainly plead guilty. And the pope has made official apologies for all that. I wasn't around at the time, of course. But if I had been, I'm sure that I, too, would have engaged in anti-Semitic behavior."

Gellar seemed to realize he was being ridiculous—although he clearly regarded the Dei medallion hanging around her neck as if it were a Nazi death's-head badge.

"You're not one of the Thirty, General, are you?"

"No," he said.

"But you'd do business with them."

"You mean with you? Yes. If Israel had relations only with its friends, we wouldn't be a country."

Serena wanted to say "Hey, I'm not Alignment," but that wouldn't carry much water here beneath the bowels of the Palace of the Grandmaster, built by the Knights of St. John, a military unit itself and cousin to the Knights Templar. All the same, she had to find out the purpose of the globes and why the Alignment would give them to the Israelis. "You're going to take these with you back to Jersualem?" she asked.

"To the place where they belong."

Serena stared at him. "You're going to rebuild the temple. You've just needed to get all the pieces together."

"Yes." Gellar was almost defiant.

"To do that, you need to remove the Dome of the Rock mosque."

"Yes."

"That would start a war with the Arabs."

"Yes."

"And you would defend yourselves, naturally."

"No," Gellar said. "You and Europe will defend us if America chooses to sit this one out. And if not, God will protect us."

"When is all this supposed to happen?"

Gellar smiled. "You had two of the globes and are the great linguist. Could you not interpret the signs?"

Serena realized she could not, but she couldn't let Gellar slip away without giving her something more. She remembered what Conrad had told her about why he'd given up his dig in Jerusalem: He couldn't figure out the astronomical alignments of the temple. Without them, he hadn't known where to dig.

"The alignments of the stars on the celestial globe don't mirror the landmarks on the terrestrial globe," she told him. "For example, there's no star on the celestial globe that mirrors Jerusalem."

"Not yet," Gellar told her with a hint of a smile. "That's why the third globe is necessary. The Hebrew prophets believed that God used the planets to give them a sign that something important was about to happen. Look closely at this globe, and you'll notice that we're in the midst of an extraordinary alignment of two symmetrical triangles formed in the sky by six planets. Do you recognize this alignment?"

"Oh my God," said Serena, seeing it clearly. "It's the Star of David."

"This is the star you were looking for over Jerusalem, Sister Serghetti," Gellar told her. "It's not a comet or a nova or a so-called star of Bethlehem. This star is the conjunction of planets that the prophet Jeremiah predicted would appear in these last days at the coming of the Messiah. It is this star to which we will align the Third Temple."

The exit door opened, and Gellar pointed the way out to her. "Thank you for returning the globes to the people of Israel, Sister Serghetti. I will take good care of them."

She stepped out of the chamber, and as soon as it closed behind her, she knew there was no turning back. A minute later, she climbed into the G55 SUV outside.

"General Gellar is Uriel," she told Benito, whose face in the mirror registered shock. "The globes are going to the Temple Mount. Surely this means war. Gellar thinks he's getting a new Jerusalem. But the Alignment is clearly betting on a new Crusade that will see them picking up all the oil and whatever else is left of the Middle East. A new Roman Empire. And that is in nobody's interest."

41

Conrad waited behind three cars in line at the Liberty Gate to Old Town. Two armored trucks flanked the gate while Greek *Evzones* in tights with submachine guns inspected every vehicle entering the fortress.

He looked at his watch: it was already three-fifteen. By now Serena had probably delivered the globes, blowing his chance to see them. Worse, he had been seen by that Dei disciple of hers, who may have warned her to exit through a different gate.

A soldier waved him up to the gate, and he handed over his license and registration slip. While the soldier ran them through a card reader, a police officer asked him questions. "Where are you going?"

"Church of St. John," Conrad lied, referring to the church across the Street of Knights from the Palace of the Grandmaster. "I'm delivering this to the icon exhibit." He glanced over his shoulder at the globe strapped precariously to the back of his seat.

"You call that an icon?" the officer said gruffly.

Conrad recovered quickly and smiled. "A replica of an icon."

The officer was still grim. "I call that an accident if it fell off your bike onto the road."

"But it didn't," Conrad said when the soldier came back with his ID.

"Firat Kayda?" the soldier said as four others circled him with their machine guns.

"Yes," Conrad said quietly.

"You're under arrest."

Conrad thought quickly as he saw a car approaching from the opposite side of the gate. "I didn't mean to steal it," he said, reaching back to the icon as he heard more than one bolt click. "I just wanted to bring it back."

He pulled the string, and the icon fell to the ground and cracked open. "Oh no!" he said.

While all eyes were diverted to the ground for a moment, he twisted the accelerator and burst through the open gate and took a sharp left behind the tower.

There were shouts and the squeal of brakes and then a delayed spray of bullets that raked the tower. Conrad hit the straightaway down the Street of Knights but saw trouble up ahead: a black S-class Mercedes sedan coming his way, leaving him little room to maneuver on either side. He'd have to cut down one of the two hundred narrow cobblestone streets and lose the police without getting lost himself.

But then he saw a second car—a silver Mercedes G-class SUV—turning out from a gate at the Palace of the Grandmaster and onto the street toward him. As it turned, he saw her in the backseat.

Serena!

Sirens blared behind him, and he glanced at his mirror to see the lights of a police car flashing from behind.

He looked back up the Street of Knights in time to swerve away from the oncoming black Mercedes, taking out the driver's-side mirror as he whooshed by.

Dead ahead was the silver Mercedes SUV. Conrad could glimpse Benito's astonished face as it passed a parked Peugeot in front of the Inn of Provence. Everything seemed to go slow-motion as Conrad considered the police behind him, the silver Mercedes ahead of him, and the parked Peugeot.

It didn't belong there.

And before he could warn Benito, the Peugeot exploded in a ball of fire and blew the Mercedes apart.

"Serena!" he shouted before the shock wave sent him flying through the air.

42

Serena found herself on her hands and knees on the street. The SUV had been split open. She tried to get up but couldn't. As she crouched there, numb from shock, she could see Benito barely moving on the other side of the burning wreck.

"Oh my God. Benito!"

She crawled on all fours toward him. Half his face was burned off, but his arm was moving. Then she saw his insides spilling out. "Oh God." She reached toward him but was still several feet away.

Benito knew he was dying and struggled for breath. "Do not be afraid, *signorina*, for he will take care of you now."

Just then a shadow fell across Benito's face, and Serena looked up to see a twisted face with an eyepatch standing over her. She screamed as the man pointed a gun at her.

"Last rites," he said in a Russian accent, and pulled the trigger.

She heard the shot but felt nothing. The assassin fell facedown in front of her. She stared in shock and heard her name.

"Serena!"

It was Conrad driving up through the smoke on a motorcycle, like a demon from hell. Behind him were the police, chasing him like the Furies.

He braked to a halt and pulled her up to her feet. "Come on."

She couldn't leave Benito. "I can't."

"Hurry," Conrad said, and dragged her by the arms and plopped her on the back of his bike. He slid in front of her and took her slack arms and wrapped them around his waist. "Please, Serena, hold on."

"I told you not to come, Conrad," she said breathlessly, bitterly, and started crying. "I told you."

"This was set up long before I got here, Serena, long before you got here." He kick-started the bike, and she could feel it roar to life beneath them. He was going to carry her away, and her work wasn't done yet.

"The council meeting tonight. I have to stay."

"I'm sorry, Serena," she heard him say as the rear tire squealed and they drove off.

43

C onrad squinted at the setting sun as he raced out the west end
of the Street of Knights into Kleovoulou Square, the police
close behind. He could feel Serena's heart pounding as she barely
held on. He turned onto the wide, shady Orpheos Street and, to
the right, spotted the wall linking the interior wall and the main
wall of Old Town. He found what he was looking for—the Gate
of St. Anthony—and rode up the ramparts, leaving the police cars
blocked below him.

He flew past the iron benches and artists drawing portraits of
tourists, scattering easels and eliciting shouts and curses. Then he
turned left into a dark tunnel.

A moment later, he burst out of Old Town through the impressive d'Amboise Gate. Two policemen started shooting as he drove
across the arched bridge and over the dry moat into the New Town.
He cut right onto Makariou Street and thundered down toward
the harbor.

"I've got a seaplane by the windmills at the breakwater," Serena said, coming to life.

"I've got a boat, I think. One of Andros's."

"I'll fly us out," she said.

There were sirens growing louder from all directions. All at once the street opened up into Kyprou Square, and he could see two triangular traffic islands in the middle of an intersection of seven streets from seven angles. There were no traffic lights, and most of the cars whizzing through were police or driven by Greek citizens.

"Hang left!" Serena shouted.

"Right," he said.

"Left as in straight ahead!"

"I know!" he shouted, and drove in the channel between the two islands to the other side, barely clearing two cars that hit their brakes.

Conrad could hear the squealing and then the crash of metal and horns behind him. In his mirror, he saw that three police cars had locked fenders.

He turned right and slowed down as he passed Starbucks and the post office and vanished into the early-evening shadows that had fallen across the seaside cafés.

At the breakwater front by the secluded windmills, Conrad could see Brother Lorenzo waiting by the Otter seaplane. The priest started to shake at the sight of him. Conrad drove up the stone pier to the edge of the water.

"They're saying a roadside bomb went off in the Knights' Quarter," Lorenzo said breathlessly as he helped Serena off the bike. "Two bodies were found."

"Benito," she told him.

Lorenzo looked at Conrad. "They said that the Israeli defense minister was the target and that the Egyptian terrorist behind it, Abdil Zawas, accidentally blew himself up. Your picture is on the television as one of his associates."

"Point that bony finger at me and I'll break it off," Conrad snapped. "What the hell are you doing here?"

Serena stopped him with a weak hand. "His instructions were always to fall back here if we ran into trouble," she said, and climbed on board and started the props.

Conrad glared at Lorenzo, who quickly followed Serena into the Otter and frantically waved him in.

Conrad rolled the motorcycle into the water, climbed into the plane, and pulled up the door behind him. Soon they lifted off into the evening sky and banked to the east as Conrad looked down to see flashing lights descend on the harbor below.

44

It was almost ten o'clock that night on Rhodes when a triumphant Roman Midas walked out onto the steps of the Palace of the Grandmaster with assorted European leaders and waited for his limousine. He was in a tuxedo after a spectacular black-tie concert outdoors in the courtyard, made all the more poignant by the violence of that afternoon's car bombing.

"Gellar and the Israelis were bloody lucky," he had heard the British prime minister tell the German chancellor before the concert. "A tragic loss for Sister Serghetti, however. Good drivers are hard to find."

"Oui" was all he heard from the French president afterward, who could understand why she'd chosen to skip the concert. "But I'm more troubled by intelligence reports that this YouTube video from Zawas signals an imminent attack on a much bigger target."

All of them had enjoyed the concert.

Some, Midas knew, more than others. While most of the dignitaries sat in chairs under the stars and listened to the Berlin

Philharmonic, seventeen of them sat in chairs under the courtyard, in the Hall of Knights, and listened to Sorath lay out the plan for world peace.

None of the faces were ones he had expected, and yet by the end of the meeting, he couldn't possibly imagine anybody else qualified to carry out the plan.

As for the plan itself, it left him in awe.

The Solomon globes were back in the hands of the Jews after so many centuries. Now General Gellar and his ultra-Orthodox friends possessed their final puzzle piece to begin construction of a Third Temple. Only the Al-Aqsa Mosque stood in their way, and Gellar was all too willing to let the Alignment do the dirty work for him and call it an act of God. All Gellar had to do was use the globes to transport the *Flammenschwert* into place beneath the Temple Mount.

There would be an uprising from the Palestinians, of course, quite likely igniting a wider war. When all reasonable avenues of diplomacy had been exhausted, which was always the case in the Arab world, the international "peace process" that Gellar had bound Israel to at this EU summit would come into play—too late for Gellar to realize that he had betrayed his country for his religion. Not that there would be room for either in the new world order. Jerusalem would be occupied by international peacekeepers, and the new temple would become the throne of the Alignment to control the Middle East.

Most amazing of all, by bringing the three Solomon globes to their final resting place, Gellar would essentially activate them at their point of origin, revealing the real prize beneath the Temple

Mount that Midas and the Alignment were after. It was a revelation greater than anything found in Judaism, Christianity, or
Islam, and the foundation of a master civilization that would sup-
plant anything that had come before in human history.

History itself would be history.

In under twenty-four hours, Midas marveled, the Jews once
again would be betrayed by thirty pieces of silver. A final Crusade
would be unleashed on the Middle East that would ensure lasting
world peace and the rise of a new Roman Empire in the twenty-
first century. All it would take was a little piece of Atlantean technology tweaked by the Nazis.

If that wasn't the final solution, Midas thought, what was?

Everything, mostly, was following the plan. Midas almost
allowed himself to smile. Then he saw Vadim pull up in the limousine. Well, almost everything.

"You look like shit, Vadim," Midas said as they drove out of the
town and into the hills toward the airstrip. "I'm amazed security let
you through. Did you get the bullet out?"

"No," Vadim grunted, clearly in pain. "But the bleeding
stopped."

"We'll take care of it after Jerusalem," Midas said. "At least
you had enough presence of mind to get out of the street after you
failed to kill Serghetti."

"The Inn of Provence is about the only one on the street with
a side door," Vadim explained. "No problem, what with the smoke
and confusion caused by Abdil's explosion."

Midas said nothing and turned on the television to watch
the BBC.

"Despite the terrorist attack on Rhodes today, the twenty-seven European foreign ministers unanimously agreed to intensify their dialogue with Israel on diplomatic issues," the big-haired anchor said. "Vice Prime Minister and Minister of Foreign Affairs Tzipi Livni said that this is a meaningful achievement for Israeli diplomacy, opening a new chapter in Israel's diplomatic relations with EU states. Israel intends to use the intensified dialogue to convince Europe to increase pressure on the Palestinians over the fate of Jerusalem and ensure that Israel's strategic interests are protected in the Middle East peace process."

Midas turned off the TV and checked his messages on his BlackBerry. He was still bothered by Vadim's failure. He'd have to get rid of Vadim as soon as he had fulfilled his purposes, two of which were still out there somewhere.

Then he saw the text from the Alignment spy code-named Dantanian.

It read: I'VE GOT THEM.

Midas smiled. It was turning out to be an even better night than he could have imagined.

45

Serena set the Otter on autopilot so she could collect herself after the devastating loss of Benito and before whatever end-of-the-world madness she and Conrad would have to deal with now. They would need to land on the water near the coast of Israel and find some way in, if they didn't get shot down first. But that was for Conrad to figure out, because she could barely think at all.

She looked over at Conrad in the copilot's seat. The entire flight, she felt him keeping one eye on her and one on Lorenzo, who was fast asleep in the rear of the cabin.

"It doesn't stop, does it, Conrad?" she asked him. "The death, the violence, the evil in this world?" She couldn't hold back anymore, and she burst into tears. "He was like a brother to me. My only real family." She started weeping uncontrollably in a way she hadn't for years. She knew Conrad had never seen her like this because *she* had never seen herself like this. Not even in her private moments. But it was as if something had broken inside.

"I can't do it, Conrad," she said. "I'm all used up. I have nothing left."

Conrad held her in his arms as best he could with their seating arrangement and brushed the wet hair away from her eyes. "What matters is what's required of us," he told her softly. "I need to know what Gellar told you."

"I told you what he told me," Serena said sharply, realizing that she wouldn't get much more in sympathy and that Conrad was right. "He wants to build a Third Temple and seems to think he's going to start very soon. The only place to build it, according to Orthodox Jews, is on the Dome of the Rock."

"Which is considered Islam's third-holiest shrine and where Al-Aqsa Mosque sits," said Conrad. "You destroy the mosque, and all hell breaks loose. I get it. Gellar gets what he wants, and the Alignment ultimately gets what it wants. But tell me about this whole Uriel thing."

"That's what doesn't make sense," she said. "In the Bible, there's an angel who guards the gate back to Eden with a flaming sword. Some traditions specifically reveal the angel's name to be Uriel."

Conrad nodded. "So you figured that Midas was bringing the *Flammenschwert* to Uriel."

"But it doesn't make sense with Gellar," she said. "He wants to destroy the Dome of the Rock and build a Third Temple for the Jews. The *Flammenschwert* turns water to fire. But there's no water in Jerusalem. No lakes, no rivers, nothing. The ancient Jews depended on precipitation from the skies, collecting rainwater in tanks and cisterns."

He looked at her and said, "You're forgetting the Gihon Spring and the network of tunnels beneath the Temple Mount."

She knew where he was going and liked to see him enthusiastic, but this wasn't realistic. "The Gihon Spring isn't really a river. That's why they call it a spring."

"It could be enough," he told her. "Back at the EU summit, Midas was pitching his mining technology as a means to extract water from the desert. Some kind of tracing technology that could reveal underground rivers and aquifers with thermal imaging."

Suddenly she saw it all. "There's going to be plenty of thermal energy after he sets off the *Flammenschwert*."

"The Temple Mount is honeycombed with well shafts, including one I've seen directly under the Dome of the Rock," Conrad told her. "All you have to do is position the *Flammenschwert* somewhere in that underground spring system, and boom—you destroy the mosque on the surface and maintain the integrity of the Temple Mount foundations. It's like a neutron bomb."

Serena said, "I suppose it would almost look like divine judgment. It's brilliant, really."

Conrad nodded. "Gellar gets his Third Temple. The Alignment gets its Crusade when it rises to defend Israel against the Arabs. And Midas gets the water and technology rights." Then he looked her in the eye. "How much do you want to bet that the warhead from the *Flammenschwert* is inside one of the globes Gellar took back to Israel? He's probably placing those globes inside some secret chamber under the Temple Mount right now."

Serena switched off the autopilot and took the steering column. "We have to warn the Israelis."

"Which Israelis?" Conrad asked her. "We could be warning the very people who are perpetrating the plan, like Gellar. We need to know for certain who's *not* Alignment, and right now, except for me and you—actually, just me—we don't even know that. We need to get to Jerusalem on our own."

"I have friends in Gaza," she said. "Catholics who helped me run food relief supplies through the blockades the Israeli coast guard set up. They could get us official work permits and fake IDs and smuggle us into Israel. I'll have to splash down within a few miles of shore, though."

"Now you're talking," he told her as she leveled off and prepared for their descent.

Then a voice from behind said, "No water landing, Sister Serghetti. You will take us to Tel Aviv."

She looked over her shoulder at Lorenzo, who had a gun pointed at her head and was glaring at Conrad.

"Now the weasel shows his true colors," Conrad said, unusually calm. "You gave me up to the police on Rhodes, didn't you? Told Midas I came so he could go and kill Serena and you could take her precious medallion?"

Serena stiffened as she felt the barrel of the gun at the back of her neck. "Lorenzo, tell me this is a moment of fear overwhelming your faith—that what Conrad said isn't true."

"Tel Aviv," Lorenzo said, waving the gun between her and Conrad. "Then you will hand me the Dei medallion before General Gellar's men take care of both of you."

"I think you should stick with your vow of silence," Conrad said.

Lorenzo pointed the gun at Conrad, pulled the trigger, and heard the click of an empty cartridge. Lorenzo frantically searched his pockets.

"I've got your bullets in here," Conrad said as he pulled out his Glock from under his shirt and shot Lorenzo in the head.

Serena didn't scream as she gripped the steering column tightly with both hands to keep herself and the Otter steady. But she shivered as she felt Lorenzo's body slide to the floor of the cockpit next to her. And the smell from Conrad's discharged Glock made her ill.

"Looks like the Dei wants you dead, Serena. You should think twice before going back to Rome."

She couldn't look at him. At either of them. She focused on bringing the Otter down for a safe landing off the waters of Gaza.

Conrad, however, was already on his phone. "Andros, it's me."

She could hear the voice on the other end shout, "Mother of God! Where are you?"

Conrad glanced at her while he talked. "I'm a few miles off the coast of Gaza. I need to get in."

"Why?" asked Andros.

Conrad said, "You see that explosion at the EU summit?"

"I told you not to come back to Greece, my friend," Andros said.

"Well, at least I got out," Conrad answered. "Now I need a ride into Gaza. You must have ships making runs here."

She couldn't make out what Andros was saying.

"Jaffa's no good," Conrad said. "Gaza. You must know someone in these waters. Someone who can meet us and take us ashore. Someone you can trust." After a minute, Conrad said, "Fine."

"Well?" she asked him when he hung up.

"Andros says he has just the man for the job. He'll meet us one kilometer due west of the breakwater at the beach north of the port."

Two hours after they splashed down, the twelve-year-old Palestinian shipowner Andros had promised finally arrived in his yellow wooden sardine boat and brought them ashore. His white T-shirt said: TODAY GAZA . . . TOMORROW THE WEST BANK AND JERUSALEM.

PART FOUR

Jerusalem

46

OHEL YITZHAK SYNAGOGUE
MUSLIM QUARTER
GOOD FRIDAY

The catering truck pulled up behind Ohel Yitzhak, or the Tent of Isaac, synagogue in the Muslim quarter of Jerusalem's Old City. General Gellar stepped out in a caterer's uniform, glanced both ways, and then gave the signal. The caterers brought out three food cases, each containing one of Solomon's three globes, and wheeled the cases on carts into the kitchen.

The elegant synagogue had been blown up by the Jordanian army in 1948. After Israel captured the Old City in the 1967 Middle East War and annexed East Jerusalem, it was finally rebuilt and rededicated in 2008. One particular modification was a secret underground passage that connected the synagogue to the Temple Mount.

The passageway was supposed to be part of a large underground complex attesting to Jewish heritage in the contested city. It was funded by the semi-governmental organization known as the Western Wall Heritage Foundation, which had signed an agreement with Jewish-American donors to maintain the Ohel

Yitzhak synagogue and the areas beneath it. Those donors had been active for decades in settling ultra-nationalist Jews in Arab areas of Jerusalem.

But General Gellar, who was on the board of the foundation, had never shared his purpose for the new passageway with his donors or submitted the final plans to the Israel Antiquities Authority for approval.

The passageway linked the synagogue with the Western Wall tunnels in the Jewish quarter. And those tunnels beneath the Western Wall in turn linked to a more ancient network unknown to either Muslims or Jews. As such, it violated Israel's promise to stop digging within the Al-Aqsa compound. After all, the last time an Israeli prime minister had opened an archaeological tunnel near the holy sites, more than eighty people had been killed in three days of Palestinian riots.

Gellar could only imagine the reaction in a few short hours when the scourge of the Temple Mount would be wiped clean by a pillar of fire that would reveal the power of the one true God.

47

Israeli troops armed with assault rifles guarded the Via Dolorosa, or the Way of Sorrows, as thousands of Christian pilgrims from around the world crowded the narrow cobblestone streets of Jerusalem's walled Old City for the traditional Good Friday procession. Some Christians even carried large wooden crosses on their shoulders along the route that Jesus was believed to have taken to His crucifixion.

Ridiculous, thought Midas, watching from the curb. He turned to Vadim, standing beside him, and said, "With the beating you've taken, you look like you could be one of the actors here."

Vadim said nothing.

"At least you're still alive." Midas looked at his BlackBerry. "It appears the Israeli coast guard found an Otter seaplane four kilometers off the coast of Gaza this morning with a dead priest inside. Bullet to the head. The Israelis say it was drug smuggling gone bad. The local rabble-rousing Catholic bishop in Gaza City says it was the trigger-happy Israeli coast guard. I say it was Yeats."

The Good Friday procession ended at the Church of the Holy Sepulcher, where tradition said Jesus was crucified and His body laid in a tomb. It was there, on Easter Sunday, that Christians would celebrate His resurrection.

Or so they believed.

The thought that the world would change in minutes, and that there was little Conrad Yeats could do about it, prompted a smile to replace Roman Midas's impatient expression as he and Vadim made their way out the Damascus Gate.

They followed the north wall of the Old City toward Herod's Gate and found an iron gate at the base of the wall. It was the cave entrance to Solomon's Quarries, a huge subterranean cavern that extended beneath the city in the direction of the Temple Mount. Inside the quarries was a secret entrance to the Temple Mount, where General Gellar would meet them.

Midas looked at his watch. It was two-thirty P.M. The first in a series of gates was about to open before him.

The cave was an official tourist site, open to the public, and a couple of Israeli policemen were outside the entrance. But today, by design, it was sealed off for a private event. It was a semiannual ceremony hosted by the Grand Lodge of the State of Israel for the benefit of Masons visiting Jerusalem during Holy Week. Non-Masons were not allowed, which kept the Good Friday crowds away.

Midas and Vadim showed the policemen their identification cards issued by the Supreme Grand Royal Arch Chapter of Israel and were allowed to step into the cave.

Midas followed a well-lit path for a hundred yards as the floor sloped down about thirty feet and opened into a cavern the size of an American football field. It was known as Freemasons' Hall, and the Masonic ceremony that Midas had hoped to avoid was under way in Hebrew and English. Twenty older gentlemen of various nationalities stood in their Masonic aprons as the Mark Master degree ceremony recounted the tale of an irregular rejected stone hewn from these very quarries that had turned out to be the cap-stone of the entrance to the temple.

But Midas already knew that. Ancient tradition said that the stones for King Solomon's First Temple were quarried here. The cavern was especially rich in white Melekeh, or royal, limestone, used in all the royal buildings. Some caves had been created by water erosion, but most had been cut by Solomon's masons.

Midas glanced up at the imposing ceiling of rock that was held up by limestone pillars just like the kind he used to make in the mines. It felt damp, and he could see beads of water trickling down the rough walls.

"Zedekiah's tears," he was told by an old Scot standing next to him. "He was the last king of Judah and tried to escape here before he was captured and carted off to Babylon. But the water comes from springs hidden all around us."

Midas and Vadim nodded, then broke away from the gathering to follow an illuminated walkway out of the cavern into one of the inner chambers separated by broad columns of limestone. There, Midas found the royal arch carved into the wall they were look-ing for and waited. A moment later, there was a faint tap. Midas

274 of TOMAS GREANIAS

tapped back twice. The outlines of an arched doorway appeared more prominently, and the stone slid open to reveal Gellar.

The only way to enter the secret tunnel, Gellar had told him, was from the inside. The irony was that Gellar was so ultra-Orthodox and regarded the Temple Mount as so holy that he refused to enter its lower chambers himself. That left the dirty job of setting off the *Flammenschwert* to Midas and Vadim.

48

From his small office near the Western Wall Plaza, Commander Sam Deker could look up and see the Dome of the Rock without the banks of monitors that helped him police the goings-on around the Temple Mount. For Jews, it was the rock on which Abraham had nearly sacrificed his son Isaac before God intervened, and later, the Holy of Holies within Solomon's Temple where the Ark of the Covenant rested. For Muslims, it was where the Prophet Muhammad had put his foot down before he ascended to heaven. For Deker, it was like the pin of a grenade placed in his hand with orders not to blow up the world.

Especially today, Good Friday.

Three weeks ago, a Palestinian construction worker had plowed a bulldozer into a crowd of young Israelis. Two weeks ago, Israeli archaeologists had accused Muslims of destroying First Temple artifacts in an attempt to erase any traces of Jewish settlements on the Temple Mount. One week ago, Christian monks had broken into a brawl at the Church of the Holy Sepulcher in advance of today's celebration.

It was always something.

A secular Jew who had grown up in Los Angeles and served with the U.S. armed forces as a demolitions specialist in the wars in Afghanistan and Iraq, Deker had been recruited by the former head of Israel's internal security service, Yuval Diskin, to work for the Shin Bet. A man who specialized in the destruction of major structures, Diskin told him, was uniquely qualified to protect one such as the Temple Mount. However, Deker quickly gathered that his chief qualification was that he was Jewish but not a real Jew, if that was possible.

For some time the Shin Bet had been concerned that Jewish extremists could attack the Temple Mount in an attempt to foil peace moves with Palestinians. It had happened before, with the assassination of Prime Minister Yitzhak Rabin, and the Shin Bet didn't want to see it again.

"The Shin Bet sees in the group we're talking about on the extreme right a willingness to use firearms in order to halt diplomatic processes and harm political leaders," Diskin told him.

Ironically, that group Deker had been warned about for so long included Israel's current defense minister, Michael Gellar, who had made a surprise appearance at the office and now stood before him.

"You saw what happened on Rhodes?" Gellar demanded. "It was intended for me."

Deker had seen it. The Egyptian Abdil Zawas had managed to blow himself up while trying to wire a roadside bomb at the European peace summit. The man wasn't a bomb maker, and it all sounded fishy to Deker. But then Zawas was always trying to outdo the ghost of his late crazy military cousin Ali, and it wouldn't surprise Deker if the Egyptian playboy had gotten in so over his head that he'd lost it.

"Greek police found evidence in the car that Abdil's real target today is the Temple Mount. Analysis of his video claiming responsibility for the attempt on my life suggests that it was an attack code to his associates in Jerusalem to detonate a nuclear device."

Deker blinked. "Today?"

"You need to seal the Temple Mount."

"You want me to seal off the Temple Mount on Good Friday and the eve of Passover?"

"Yes."

"But that means closing off the Western Wall to worshippers, ticking off both Jews and Christians. That's on top of the Arabs, who are always mad."

"I know what it means, Deker." General Gellar was pulling rank. "You need to check all access points and your informants. Things the security feeds don't pick up."

Deker nodded, typed an alert on his BlackBerry, and then put it away.

"What did you just do?" Gellar demanded.

"I sent a quick 140-character text through Twitter to my network."

"Is that secure?"

"Yes and no."

The BlackBerry chirped, and Deker looked at the feeds and frowned. The guide at the Gihon Springs was reporting that a man and woman had gone into Hezekiah's Tunnel but never emerged from the tunnel exit at the Siloam Pool.

He called up the video, and as he watched the monitor, he watched Gellar. The blood from the general's face drained.

"That's Conrad Yeats and Serena Serghetti. Abdil's associates."

Yeats, maybe, thought Deker, who had heard plenty of stories in his days with the armed forces. Sister Serghetti, Mother Earth herself, never. Perhaps Yeats had abducted her at gunpoint and forced her to help.

Deker radioed Elezar, who was monitoring Warren's Shaft near Hezekiah's Tunnel. "Anything on the intruders?"

The radio crackled. "They're in the tunnels," Elezar reported. "Under the Temple Mount."

"Tell the Yamam unit to assemble in the Map Room right away." Deker turned to Gellar. "Too late to seal the Temple Mount now."

49

HEZEKIAH'S TUNNEL
JEWISH QUARTER

Serena knew that ancient cities couldn't exist without a water source, and Jerusalem was no exception. The City of David had developed around the only real water source in the area, the Gihon Spring, which ran through the bottom of the Kidron Valley. During the Assyrian and Babylonian attacks, King Hezekiah had constructed an aqueduct through which the waters could be hidden inside the city, an extraordinary engineering feat at the time.

It was through this tunnel that Serena followed Conrad through waist-high water in the dark with only one flashlight to guide them. It was all their driver from Gaza had on hand. They had been greeted at the beach north of Al Gaddafi by a van from the local Catholic church, which drove them up Salahadeen Road to the Erez industrial zone and the border gate with Israel. The Israeli official at the checkpoint had looked over their bogus work permits, which Serena had insisted would give them a better chance of getting into Israel than the underground smuggling tunnels, which Israeli warplanes bombed almost daily. A long minute later, the soldiers had waved them through. They had crossed the 1950 Armistice Line into Israel and driven toward Jerusalem, only forty-eight miles away.

The drive from Gaza had ended in Silwan, a poor Arab village of cinder-block houses crumbling down the hillsides to the Gihon Spring at the bottom of the Kidron. There, Serena found the Fountain of the Virgin and the church commemorating the spot where Mary once drew water to wash the clothes of Jesus. It was almost one P.M. and a Friday, so the caretaker was about to close the gate. But Conrad gave him a tip, and he let them descend the stone steps into the spring's cave.

It was here that Serena's expertise was exhausted and she had to trust Conrad's knowledge of Jerusalem's underbelly. But sloshing through the ever rising water, she was beginning to have doubts.

Hezekiah's Tunnel was a third of a mile long, mostly under three feet wide, and in some places, under five feet high. The caretaker at the entrance had warned them that the water was knee-high today and the walk would take them about forty minutes before they exited at the Pool of Siloam. Conrad, however, told her that they would be exiting halfway through, at the point where the tunnel took an odd S-shaped course through the rock. This was where Hezekiah's Tunnel branched from the tunnel leading from the Gihon Spring to the bottom of Warren's Shaft.

The tunnel had narrowed, and the dirty water was now waist-high. Serena bumped her head against the ceiling of the tunnel, which had started to slope sharply. The water was now up to her neck.

"The ceiling is lowest here, under five feet high, and the water level highest," Conrad told her. "So you'll have to hold your breath."

He took her by the hand, and they walked forward until their heads were underwater. They walked about three feet before the tunnel ceiling started to rise and their heads surfaced.

They were in a different tunnel, the water level dropping rapidly, and they soon reached a stone platform on the edge of a giant precipice. Serena felt chilled to the bone and wrung her dripping hair like a towel to squeeze out the water. When she looked down, she saw what looked like a giant subway tunnel with wide white limestone steps descending into the depths of the earth. She said, "This looks like the grand gallery of the Great Pyramid in Egypt."

Conrad nodded. "Why do you think Solomon married all those Egyptian princesses? To gain access to the sand hydraulic technology that built the pyramids. Except what he did here was amazing. He inverted the design so that everything you know is upside down."

That's crazy, she thought. But now that he mentioned it, the tunnel made sense.

Conrad said, "You know that shaft I was telling you about under the Dome of the Rock?"

She craned her head up and saw the opening in the ceiling overhead. It appeared to go all the way up to the top of the Temple Mount. "I thought I felt a draft."

"Back when the First Temple was up there, the top of the shaft was capped with a platform on which the Ark of the Covenant could be lowered during a siege," he told her. "Here, take this."

She looked down in her palm and saw a brick of C4 explosive. "Where on earth did you get this?"

"From the driver of your Sunday-school van in Gaza," he told her. "Now climb up on my shoulders and stick this inside the mouth of the shaft. We need to close it off in case we fail to stop the *Flammenschwert*. Otherwise, a geyser of fire is going to incinerate that mosque."

She took his hand, put a boot on his knee, and stepped onto his shoulders until her head was inside the bottom of the shaft. She planted the C4 on the wall of the shaft and jumped back down onto the stone platform.

She said, "You gave us only twenty minutes on the fuse."

"Insurance that we close the shaft to the surface before the *Flammenschwert* goes off," he explained. "The important thing is to make sure the mosque is still standing on the surface. Without Arab uprisings in the streets, Gellar can't justify the disproportionate Israeli response that will ignite a wider war. Whatever happens down below here is, well, secondary."

She looked down into the great gallery below. "The King's Chamber is down at the bottom, isn't it?"

"Right." He pulled out his Glock, the one he had killed Lorenzo with, and checked the clip. "So are the globes, the *Flammenschwert*, and God knows what else."

50

With a full-blown national emergency under way, Commander Sam Deker of the Israeli Shin Bet had no trouble assembling the elite five-member counter-terrorism unit known as the Yamam. They were beneath the temple in under six minutes.

They gathered inside the top-secret Map Room, itself a national secret. The chamber looked like a flight briefing room, with theater-style seating for six in front of computer consoles and a nine-by-twenty-four-foot curved screen with 160-degree views. Each officer carried the standard M4 assault rifle with a Glock 21 .45 sidearm.

"We all follow the plan used in the Taibe raid a few years ago," Deker told them. "We're to capture or kill an armed group hidden in the tunnels below us and secure a device that may be nuclear in nature before it goes off. I cannot overemphasize how grave this threat is to the Temple Mount and the very existence of Israel."

High-definition three-dimensional images of the tunnel system filled the screen. In addition to live security feeds, the computer models used military flight-simulator technology to enable virtual remote viewing around the tunnels. Gellar in particular preferred a remote hookup. Being Orthodox, he refused to walk the holy limestone tunnels himself, leaving it to impure types like Deker.

"Four security zones make up the Temple Mount in descending order: this Map Room, Solomon's Hall, the King's Chamber, and the four River Gates region. We pair in three teams of two. Team One stations itself here. Team Two stations itself in the King's Chamber and monitors access to the River Gates. Team Three patrols the tunnels. Shoot to kill anybody who is not in this room. Should you exit the tunnels alive, you will not speak of this again."

The faces he saw understood him perfectly. Yamam forces specialized in both hostage-rescue operations and offensive takeover raids against targets in civilian areas such as the Temple Mount. Most of their activities were classified, and their success was credited to other units. Most important to Deker, they answered to the civilian Israeli police forces rather than the military, although most came exclusively from Israeli special forces units.

"Let's go," Deker said.

As the unit prepared to disperse, the officer who had been paired with Deker called him over to his console. "There's something you should see, sir," he said.

Apparently, the officer had been curious enough to research the construction of the Map Room and had called up the names of the A-list experts who had consulted on the project with the Israel Antiquities Authority and the UCLA Urban Simulation Team in the United States.

The top archaeologist on the list was Conrad Yeats.

"Looks like Yeats kept or cut a tunnel or two for himself," Deker said, red-faced. "If it's not on the map, it's not on the camera. We're going to have to move out with the others."

"There's more, sir," the officer said. "The shaft plugs to secure the tunnels were manufactured by an Israeli company based at the Tefen Industrial Park. It's a subsidiary of Midas Minerals & Mining."

Deker frowned. "The Midas conglomerate?"

"Yes, sir. And it appears that General Gellar has an interest in the Tefen subsidiary. What does it mean?"

Deker heard a thud and turned to see two Yamam on the floor and the rest gasping for breath. He smelled almonds in the air and realized it was cyanide gas. The door to the chamber was closing from the top down, and Deker knew that anybody trapped inside would die.

"Gellar has betrayed us!" Deker shouted, and made a flying leap for it.

51

The *Flammenschwert* was gone.

Conrad stood with Serena inside the King's Chamber—an expansive vault in the shape of a perfect one-by-two rectangle, its height of forty cubits exactly half the length of its eighty-cubic floor diagonal. In the center of the stone floor stood the three globes, but the armillary globe was split open like an empty womb. On each of the chamber's four walls was a towering archway, each leading down its own tunnel.

Four tunnels, two people, little time, Conrad thought. The *Flammenschwert* could have been taken down any one of the four shafts.

But Serena was already ahead of him, reading the ancient Hebrew letters over the archways, trying to figure out which tunnel to take, because they'd only have one shot.

"This is incredible," she said. "Do you know what these say?"

"I have my suspicions," he told her. "The star shafts of an inverted pyramid obviously can't point to the heavens. So I figured there weren't any beneath the Temple Mount. These are well shafts."

"Each one leads to a different river," she said. "Their names are written in some kind of Proto-Semitic language. It's practically pre-Atlantean. That door says Tigris, that one says Euphrates, that one over there says Pishon, and this one here says—"

"Gihon," Conrad said. "The four rivers of Eden. So Uriel is the angel with the flaming sword at the gate of Eden after all."

Serena said, "But Eden was in Mesopotamia, where the ancient Babylonian civilization originated."

Eden was like Atlantis, Conrad knew. Everybody had a different idea about where it could be, and archaeological evidence to back it up. But Jewish legend pinpointed the land of Israel as one distinct possibility. What seemed to throw off most archaeologists was the second chapter of Genesis, which described four separate rivers in the Land of Eden that shared a common headwater source. Only two were ever found—the Tigris and the Euphrates. Nobody had discovered the rivers Pishon or Gihon. But Genesis never said all four rivers were aboveground.

"Mesopotamia is just where the Tigris and Euphrates empty out," Conrad told her. "Their headwater source could be down here somewhere, along with the underground waterways of the Pishon and the Gihon."

"Genesis does refer to underground waterways providing water to the surface," she said, the linguist in her apparently rising to the surface. "The original Hebrew word is 'springs.' Genesis says the springs came up from the earth and watered the whole surface of the ground. And the Book of Revelation says that at the end of time, those four rivers will flow out from the temple."

Conrad closed the armillary globe and locked its two hemispheres in place. He could feel Serena's stare as he began to adjust the dial that controlled a tiny marker in the spiral groove representing the motion of the sun.

"This works just like the observatory deck at the Temple of the Water Bearer in Atlantis and the west patio of the U.S. Capitol," he said. "The only difference is that this deck is underground. You can't look at the skies with your naked eye to mark the position of the sun in relation to the stars. You have to use these globes."

"Gellar said the armillary uses planetary geometry," Serena said.

"It does," he said. "The planets align to form the Star of David. Which was how the Israelis got their national symbol in the first place. It's astrologically derived, just like the fish symbol of the early Church in the age of Pisces. Anyway, the trick is to follow the path of the sun across the alignment until X marks the spot. In this case, it's a location beneath the Temple Mount."

"Uriel's Gate," Serena said all of a sudden. "The gate to paradise. That's where Midas has taken the *Flammenschwert.*"

"Eureka." Conrad checked the clip in his Glock again and rammed it back in. The click broke Serena's trance; she stared at the gun and at him. Which was what he'd intended. "The sun marker points to the Gihon shaft to reach Uriel's Gate," he said.

"You have to be sure, Conrad."

"This isn't a panel discussion at some conference. Look around you. We're in an ancient chamber deep beneath the Temple Mount with three globes and four doorways. The Gihon Spring of Jerusalem obviously has its source in the same Gihon River of Eden."

He stopped and stared at the gateway marked Gihon.

"That's it, Serena. That's the revelation of the globes: The Temple Mount guards the gate to Eden."

"The River of Life," Serena said. "The properties in the water contain the building blocks of life on earth."

Conrad nodded. "This is what Midas was after all along, what all the money in the world can't buy him: life. He's using the *Flammenschwert* to light the Gihon ablaze and trace it back to its headwater source."

"And at the same time destroy the Dome of the Rock," Serena said.

Conrad heard another click of a Glock, but it wasn't his. He looked up at Serena, who was staring over his shoulder, and then heard a voice say, "Hands up, Yeats."

Slowly, Conrad turned to see an Israeli soldier pointing a gun at him—Sam Deker. Conrad knew him from his earlier digs at the Temple Mount. A good if humorless man.

"It's your boss you should be after, Deker," Conrad said.

Deker kept the gun trained on him. "What makes you sure Gellar is involved?"

"Because he told me," Serena said when a bullet struck Deker in the shoulder.

Conrad turned to see Vadim pop up from the entry of the Gihon Gate. He made a grab for Serena, and she screamed as he pulled her down into the hellhole.

"Serena!" Conrad shouted and ran over to the tunnel as a flurry of bullets flew up at him from the dark. He dove for cover. Breathing hard, he realized that Midas and Vadim were one step ahead of him—the final step. They must have removed the *Flammenschwert* from its globe and were preparing to detonate it at the source of the Gihon below. And now they had Serena.

"There's another way down to the Gihon," said Deker, who was sitting up against another wall, his hand on his shoulder, blood seeping through his fingers.

"Oh, so now you're convinced that I'm not with Gellar?"

"Just tell me what you're really after, Yeats."

Conrad said, "Stopping Armageddon. Midas has an incendiary weapon that's about to ignite the Gihon and everything on the surface. I have to stop it, and you have to go back up and stop Gellar if I fail."

"You know how to dispose of a nuclear device? Because that's what I do," Deker said. "Maybe I should go down and you go back up."

"It's not exactly a nuke, but I can disarm it," Conrad said. "But I can't disarm Gellar if I go up. Or stop your government from overreacting after the Arabs overreact if the Dome of the Rock blows."

Deker nodded to the Pishon Gate on the other wall. "You can take that shaft down to the end and turn right. Follow the riverbank, and it will lead you to the two pillars by the Gihon."

Conrad helped Deker to his feet and then made his way to the Pishon Gate. He looked back inside the King's Chamber. Deker had already disappeared back up to Solomon's Stairway, and Conrad realized that he had forgotten to tell Deker about the C4 under the Dome of the Rock well shaft.

No matter, Conrad thought as he started down the shaft. Deker had as much chance of reaching the surface as Conrad had in reaching the *Flammenschwert* in time to stop it.

52

Midas was with the *Flammenschwert* at the banks of the Gihon River when Vadim and Serena emerged from the two pillars that guarded the entrance of the tunnel back up into the Temple Mount.

"Behold the Gihon," Midas told her with a sweeping gesture across the vast subterranean cavern. He made a show of punching in the activation code on the instrument panel. The display lit up as the *Flammenschwert* came to life.

The timer counted down from 6:00 . . . 5:59 . . . 5:58 . . .

Midas let out a sigh of relief. He had done it. He had obtained the Sword of Fire. He had found the gate to Eden and the primordial waters of life on earth, the waters that could heal his fatal neurological condition and let him live forever. The very River of Life that had scared even the God of Genesis. Now Midas would blow it open and restore paradise on earth.

The old order would pass. The old religions would be swept away in the cleansing fire of Armageddon. Then the cool water of the new world order would come. And he would control it. He, the Water Bearer. Truly, this would be the Age of Aquarius. The age of Pisces and the Church was over.

"Vadim," he called. "It's time." He motioned Vadim over to the *Flammenschwert* and watched him take it to the water.

"It's going to work like this, Sister Serghetti," Midas said, digging his gun into her side. "The *Flammenschwert* will ignite the water. The heat will force it to rise like a coil through the well shaft you just emerged from, gather steam from the chambers above, and ultimately spew out fire like a geyser, destroying everything topside. It could alter geography significantly. In fact, I think that's what this whole complex was built to do, like some sort of geothermal machine."

"I know how it works, Midas. I've seen it before."

Midas said nothing for a moment, making sure Vadim launched the *Flammenschwert* into the water correctly. The casing assembly floated by itself, an amber light blinking six times before burning a steady red.

Serena said, "Hope you've got a place to hide when this blows, Midas, because you're going to fry when it does."

"As a matter of fact, I do," Midas said, then barked his final order to Vadim. "You stay with the *Flammenschwert* until the two-minute mark. Then you can join us in the Map Room. It should be clear by now."

Vadim looked unsure about staying behind but nodded.

Midas could feel Serena shaking as he pushed her back toward a stone stairway she hadn't seen before. "The Map Room, above the King's Chamber, is separated from the main line and closed off. We'll ride out the chaos for a few days and then emerge into a new world."

Midas knew Serena was smart enough to accept that he was going to kill her, but she would go along with him in the vain hope that her beloved Conrad Yeats would come to the rescue. Midas doubted that. But just in case, he would keep her close.

"I see what Gellar thinks he's going to get out of this, Midas," she said as they began to ascend the narrow stairwell. "And I see what the Alignment is sure it will get out of this. But I don't see what you get out of blowing up the Dome of the Rock."

"That's not what I'm blowing up, Sister Serghetti. I'm blowing up what is at the other end of the Gihon River, buried deep beneath us. The very Gate to Eden. The primordial waters of life itself. If you can live forever, you don't need heaven. You don't need God. Because you are a god."

"You know, Lucifer had that problem. He confused himself with the Creator."

Midas laughed, but then the steps started to shake from an explosion high above. He felt an elbow in his gut as Serena tried to push him down the steps. He recovered swiftly and gave her a blow across the face with his gun. She cried out in pain.

"I'm in control," he hissed in her ear. "Soon the world will know it."

She said nothing in the dark, but he could hear her breathing.

He was pushing her forward when he heard a gunshot back at the Gihon. Then the voice of Conrad Yeats rang out.

"Vadim bit the big vitamin, Midas. I've got a deal for you: the *Flammenschwert* for Serena."

53

URIEL'S GATE

Conrad stood dripping wet by the banks of the underground river. The *Flammenschwert* warhead he had retrieved from the water was on the stone platform next to Vadim's body. The timer was down to three minutes and counting.

How the hell am I going to deactivate this thing? he wondered as he began to unscrew the casing of the sphere with the blade of his knife. Then he thought better of it and stopped. *Maybe all I have to do is keep this out of the water when it explodes.*

He folded his knife, picked up his gun, and stood up as Midas emerged with Serena from a tunnel. Midas had one hand wrapped around Serena's throat and the other pointing a gun at her chest, using her like a shield.

"Drop the gun," Midas said. "Or I kill her."

"Don't do it, Conrad. Shoot me and Midas both. Save the Temple Mount."

Conrad saw the strength in her eyes. She was ready to die. But *he* wasn't ready for her to die. "I can't lose you again."

Midas smiled. "Then you'll drop it."

Conrad put his gun on the ground, reminding himself that all he had to do was keep Serena alive and the *Flammenschwert* out of the water.

"Kick the gun into the water," Midas ordered.

Conrad gave it a swipe with his foot and it skidded to the edge of the river and stopped.

That was good enough for Midas, who said, "Take the *Flammenschwert* and set it back into the water where it belongs. Hurry."

"No, Conrad!" Serena shouted. "If you do what Midas wants, you can kiss any hope of peace in the Middle East goodbye. Me, too. Let me go and save the world—for me."

Conrad hesitated. Something had changed in her eyes.

"I understand, Conrad," Serena said calmly as she put her hand on top of Midas's gun. "Let me help you."

She forced Midas's hand, and the gun exploded. She collapsed, exposing a stunned Midas as he staggered back a step and raised his gun to shoot Conrad.

"No!" Conrad shouted, diving for his gun and shooting Midas between the eyes. The bullet blew Midas's skull against the stone wall, killing him instantly.

Conrad ran to Serena. Her shirt was soaked in blood. It was pumping out of her chest.

"Oh, God, no." He ripped the shirt open to see the bullet hole above her left breast. Right above her heart. "No!"

He put his hands on the wound to try and stop the bleeding. Then he felt her hand on his and looked into her eyes. The light in them was fading.

"Take Uriel's sword, Conrad. Back to the King's Chamber. It can't explode in the water."

"There's water seeping through the stones all over this place, Serena. Every chamber is like an empty oil drum. You can't tell me that it still won't ignite this river."

"No, but the impact might not be so bad if it's not immersed."

"I can't leave you."

She shook her head. "No time . . ."

"Serena," he said, trying to lift her, but even more blood came out. "I can't."

"What's the clock say?"

He looked at the readout. "Ninety seconds."

"You know the Book of Revelation?" she said.

"I know," he said. "You read the ending. The Church wins."

"No," she said. "God wins. There is no Church in the New Jerusalem. No temples or mosques, either. Just God and his people."

"That's great," said Conrad. "But what do I do in the meantime without you?"

She didn't answer. Her body was limp.

"Serena!" he said, shaking her. "Serena!"

He looked at the timer on the *Flammenschwert*: 57 seconds . . . 56 seconds . . .

He wiped his hands, lifted the device, and then took off with it for the shaft. At the bottom of the steps, he looked back and saw Serena's lifeless body on the floor of the river cave.

Four granite slab doors inside the King's Chamber were already beginning to drop by the time Conrad reached the armillary globe and placed the *Flammenschwert* inside. He barely slipped under the falling slab into the Gihon shaft before it shut. Then he ran back down the steps to Uriel's Gate. The timer started to beep at the thirty-second count . . . 29 seconds . . . 28 seconds . . .

He burst past the pillars into the cave. Serena's body lay on the banks where he'd left her. He collapsed next to her, pulling her into his arms.

"I stopped him," he told her, though he knew she couldn't hear him. He looked at the hole above her blood-soaked breast and wept. "Oh, God, no. Please, no."

He lifted her into his arms and carried her to the torrent, the beeping of the timer counting down audibly to zero. A terrific quake shook the entire Temple Mount as the *Flammenschwert* exploded in the upper chamber. Chunks of rock began to fall around him, making huge splashes in the river.

Holding Serena in his arms, he jumped into the rushing waters as flames burst out of the Gihon shaft. Sheets of fire flickered like waves in the air above the river, illuminating Serena's face as if she were an angel beneath the surface.

As the current carried them both away, Conrad kissed her goodbye with his last breath. The river sucked them down a dark tunnel. He tried to hold on to her, but her hand slipped away. He shouted out to her in the water, but then his head hit a rock and everything went black.

54

It was just after three o'clock, and General Gellar was praying at the Western Wall, his head covered with his yarmulke and his shoulders draped with his silk tallith, when the explosion rocked the Temple Mount.

There were screams and shouts, and he looked up at the Dome of the Rock to behold the pillar of fire he had dreamed of for so long. But it didn't come, and the shaking began to die down like a small earthquake. There were no aftershocks.

Confused and disturbed by what this could mean, he slowly made his way across the crowds in the plaza who were engaged in animated discussion over what had just happened.

As he approached the curb, a white van pulled up and a door slid open to reveal a bleeding Commander Sam Deker and several armed Yamam. Gellar tried to turn but felt something prick his neck as he blacked out.

* * *

Several hours later, Deker and his team stormed the labs of the Israeli subsidiary of Midas Minerals & Mining at the Tefen Industrial Park near the Lebanese border. After the raid, he met with his U.S. counterparts in one of the theaters on the corporate campus. Marshall Packard was sitting on a chair on the stage, reading over a report with a tall, thin woman who introduced herself as Wanda Randolph.

"Hell, Deker, this month alone they had engineers from Intel, Siemens, Exxon, and MIT visiting the R & D center to learn about this new water detection and extraction technology," Packard told him. "How could the Israelis not know Gellar had an ownership interest in the company?"

"Many members of the government and military have similar arrangements with the companies here."

Packard frowned. "You secured the rest of those metal pellets in the labs?"

"Destroyed." Deker held his ground. "I trusted neither my superiors nor you to properly dispose of them."

"That's unfortunate," Packard said. "Just one of those little fire beads could have unlocked Atlantean technology."

Deker said nothing.

"What are you going to say about Gellar in your report to the Israeli prime minister?"

"That he died a hero of Israel, preventing what could have been a debilitating strike on the Temple Mount. Had it succeeded, it would have triggered a war in which Israel would have prevailed, of course, but at the cost of many lives."

"What about the globes? I don't suppose they could have possibly survived."

"If they did, I wouldn't tell you," Deker said. "I'm more concerned about Yeats and Serghetti. Any word on their fate?"

Packard looked somber. "No," he said. "But wherever they are, I think it's time we finally leave them the hell alone."

That evening Deker returned to the Western Wall and looked for the slip of paper with the prayer on it that Gellar had inserted between the massive rocks. It was taboo, but Deker wasn't much of a devout Jew.

Using what he had seen from the surveillance footage, he found what he was reasonably certain was the prayer.

Come let us go up the mountain of
the Lord, that we may walk the
paths of the Most High.
And we shall beat our swords into ploughshares,
and our spears into pruning hooks.
Nation shall not lift up sword against nation—
Neither shall they learn war any more.
And none shall be afraid, for the mouth of the
Lord of Hosts has spoken.

It was a good prayer, Deker thought. He was sure he had heard it somewhere before in his childhood. Seeing the Jews and Christians around him praying, and hearing the distant call of the minaret for Muslims to pray as well, he decided to repeat that prayer as his way of saying kaddish for the souls of Conrad Yeats and Serena Serghetti.

55

It was already hot at ten A.M. on Easter Sunday when Reka Bressler, a grad student from Hebrew University's Orion Center for the Study of Dead Sea Scrolls, led her American tour group past a stone marker that said SEA LEVEL to the rocks of the Dead Sea over four hundred yards below.

The desolate area was the lowest point on earth, an otherworldly landscape of sheer cliffs, caves, and rocks around the waters. It was believed to be the site of several biblical cities, including Sodom and Gomorrah, or rather, what was left of them. Indeed, it looked like the aftermath of a nuclear explosion, and the smell of sulfur didn't help.

But the water of the Dead Sea was supposed to possess therapeutic powers. Already a couple from her group had jumped in to test the salty sea's legendary buoyancy. One American, settling comfortably in the water, looked like he was reclining on an invisible lawn chair as he scanned the *Jerusalem Post.*

That was when Reka saw the body of a fully clothed man washed up on the beach. He was clearly no tourist. She cursed and ran down the shore to him and turned him over.

His face was caked with blood. His head must have struck a rock somewhere. She bent down, placed two fingers on his neck, and felt a faint pulse. She pressed on his stomach, and he spat up water. She was about to give him mouth-to-mouth when she felt a hand on her shoulder.

"That's okay, I've got him."

Reka rose and saw a woman in torn clothes with a scorched medallion on her chest. There was something familiar and ethereal about her. But the footprints behind her proved that she was just as flesh-and-blood as her companion. "But you look worse than he does," Reka said.

The woman smiled. "I'll be sure to tell him. He'll like that. You may want to get back to your group. I think there's a man under that hand waving a newspaper above the surface of the water."

"*Harah*," Reka muttered, and started running down the beach.

Serena held Conrad's head in her arms as he coughed, blinked his eyes open, and looked at her and then at the seemingly god-forsaken place around them.

"This can't be hell, because you're here," he said.

She saw him staring at the scorched medallion hanging from her neck. Her Shekel of Tyre had been sheared in half by the bullet it had deflected, searing her chest with a cauterized flesh wound in the shape of a crescent moon. "River of Life, Conrad."

He sat up and wrapped his arms around her. "Thank you, God."

She wiped the tears from her eyes, and then she removed the medallion from her neck. "Well, I'm not returning to Rome."

Conrad looked at her. "Where are you going?"

"Wherever you go, Conrad."

"You sure you want to do this?"

"I do."

"And then?"

"We can love God, serve others, be fruitful, and multiply."

"Well, let's not be disobedient, then," he said, and kissed her under the beating sun.

ACKNOWLEDGMENTS

Special thanks to my amazing editor, Emily Bestler, and my unflinching agent, Simon Lipskar, for their insight and support. To my publisher, Judith Curr, at Atria for her enthusiasm and genius, and to Sarah Branham and Laura Stern for keeping everything running on time—even me. Thanks also to Louise Burke, Lisa Keim, and the world-class team at Pocket responsible for getting my books out to the farthest corners of the earth.

I'm incredibly fortunate to have the marketing support of such creative individuals from Simon & Schuster as Kathleen Schmidt, David Brown, Christine Duplessis, and Natalie White. Also Doug Stambaugh at S&S Digital, Tom Spain at S&S Audio, and Kate-Lyall Grnat in the UK. Thank you all.

I owe a debt of gratitude to those individuals within the intelligence communities of the United States, Europe, and the Middle East who plied me with Mojitos in hopes I'd forget certain parts of our conversations and their real names. Done. Thank you for generously sharing your unique perspectives on world peace.

Thanks, finally, to the Israel Antiquities Authority, the Jordanian Waqf, and members of certain nongovernmental organizations on either side of the Temple Mount divide in Jerusalem who share a passion for the protection of the holy places.